PRAISE FOR RICHARD WIRICK'S
ONE HUNDRED SIBERIAN POSTCARDS

"A brilliant idea, brilliantly executed."
—HUGO WILLIAMS, *Times Literary Supplement*

"Richard Wirick is an insurance lawyer with the soul—
and the pen—of a poet."
—ANNA REID, author of *Borderland: A Journey
through the History of Ukraine*

"Richard Wirick's deeply felt, beautifully written palm-of-
the hand-tales that make up *One Hundred Siberian Postcards* are as luminous as Basho's *Narrow Road to Oku* and
as moving as the Hemingway vignettes of *In Our Time.*
Yet Wirick's profoundly moving book is unlike anything
else I've read; an ode to Siberia as much as it is to
the human condition."
—SAMANTHA GILLISON, author of *The King of America*

"Attentive and compassionate, Richard Wirick has
journeyed through Siberia and returned *with it said.*"
—JOHN WITTE, editor of *Northwest Review*

Papaver somniferum L.

KICKING IN

STORIES

RICHARD WIRICK

Soft Skull Press
New York

This is a work of fiction. Names, characters, places, and incidents are the product of the author's imagination or are used fictitiously. Any resemblance to actual persons, living or dead, is entirely coincidental.

Library of Congress Cataloging-in-Publication Data
Wirick, Richard.
  Kicking in : stories / Richard Wirick.
     p. cm.
  ISBN 978-1-59376-280-3 (alk. paper)
  I. Title.

  PS3623.I75K53 2010
  813'.6—dc22

                              2009050390

Interior design by Elyse Strongin, Neuwirth & Associates, Inc.

Printed in the United States of America

Soft Skull Press
An Imprint of COUNTERPOINT LLC
2117 Fourth Street
Suite D
Berkeley, CA 94710

Distributed by Publishers Group West

10   9   8   7   6   5   4   3   2   1

All the conventions conspire
To make this fort assume
The furniture of home;
Lest we should see where we are,
Lost in a haunted wood,
Children afraid of the night
Who have never been happy or good.

W. H. AUDEN, "SEPTEMBER 1, 1939"

To Anthony Robinson, Dean Ferguson,
and Kenneth Dekleva
First readers and goodly *frères*
This book be given

CONTENTS

• CONTENTS •

HARDIN STREET

GIVEN MY ever-present love trouble, it was the last thing I needed to have happen that awful spring, the coldest in the city in years. But who is ever ready for a client who has put an irate customer in the car-painting kiln and turned it on until she cooks? It was more a massacre than a case, one of those half-baked mayhems Kiley pushed off on me so as not to embarrass himself in his final year before partnership.

Still, it was made worse by my heart's condition: the third of my unwise, foul, and unnatural office flings, with someone (Bari was her name, redheaded, a sphinx) I had only shaken hands with weeks before at the new associates party. Waiting to talk to Kiley now, I looked down two floors to where Bari's entire office floated like a golden cage against the olive reflecting panels of the neighboring building. Her back was to me, all that glass and wind and silence between us. She'd called me down the morning after our third night together, handed me the jacket I'd left at her house, and that had been it.

Her failure to explain this and her scratching her nose now as I watched made her all the more magnificent. She ran her whole head along her finger, back and forth like corn on the cob. And her stockings—seams in back—and her neck arched high, and her long, smoky legs at an angle. This last thing concentrated my grief like a tiny burning star down along my ribs, and when it jumped into my throat I thought how my sad, flat heart, which had let her all out and lost her like a flubbery tire, was never more mine.

I was saying to myself how I could never have known. *How bad was that candy, I could never have known.*

The woman had been burned over 60 percent of her body. Most of it was on her arms and hands, which she'd put all along the wall and, eventually, up against the door once she realized what was happening. But she'd lived, and according to Kiley this was all we needed for a defense. The medical files were spread out between us on his desk. His chair squeaked as he spun around, lifting the skin graft negs to the window.

"I'm not saying she's going to be the next Christie Brinkley, but these plastics doctors can work miracles. They took one of these wild polio kids and straightened his leg out just like that four iron."

His pointing arm stayed in the air an extra second or two while I didn't laugh.

"She was out of that kiln in three minutes, soon as they knew what was happening."

"It wasn't like that," I ventured. "People don't *wander in*. It was like, I think, they had to have *done* it."

He tilted a photo. "Negligence. Accident. People make mistakes."

"The profiles of the kids, they seem kind of rough—"

"The kids were new. They can't be watching everything."

"Michael," I said. I had this with him, this latitude somehow. Anyone else would have been cowering at his gaze.

"Go *down* there. Just go there, drive down this afternoon. I'd go with you, but my trainer's coming in."

He slid the files to me, surprisingly gently. Why had I never noticed *his* squint before? Were all of us squinting now? Was that what we were coming to? But Bari's, really, was different from this, more curious and human, with those soft gobs of eyes.

A picture had fallen down under the desk. It wasn't a

negative, but a fully developed photo—an enlargement of a skin graft, what must have been her arm. The black and white skin looked like land seen from an airplane. Over it all was a thin film of fog, the rising and hardening bubbles of scars.

When I got back to my office, I immediately had to brace myself. She'd passed me in the hall on the way to see Kiley. (I knew she was working for him, but they hid it from their client, old plane engine manufacturers from Mobile, to whom women were secretaries, or less than that—"girls.")

I felt like my whole desk was going to rise up. Or worse, as if it would vibrate, like in the after-ripples of a temblor. I'd had these spells a lot lately and gotten a Valium prescription. But I was out of fives and tens now, and the pharmacist was away. What did it, I think, was the finality of her eyes; the red, red eyebrows; the red Cheops hair. Surely, they were mild things to the disinterested world, but to me they were fire pokers, mounds of red ants.

My book of business was nothing to brag about. All of it fit on the top of my desk. I went through a few files to postpone even calling, even having to talk to the car-painting kids. Choy's Mobile Lunch was sending a lot of cases, and American Dust Bag and Pure Power Gym. Choy's was a restaurant, a three-trailer chain. Slip-and-falls and grease spray had always been my staple, but lately I'd been getting more bug eggs cases. Cluster after cluster of silvery larvae were getting past the lettuce man and onto people's plates. One guy got through two or three spoonfuls, thinking it was some kind of haute potato salad.

At their depositions, bug-egg eaters relived the whole shebang. They all had the same lawyer, who had it scripted clean: plaintiff grabs his neck, shakes his free arm, pops his eyes. Many now lived with weird salad phobias, pure cold terror at the green of the leaf.

American Dust Bag's vacuum sacks exploded—upward through the handle column into peoples' faces or down in silent, flaking turds across the white carpets of suburban living rooms. Only one in every thousand and then one in every *ten* thousand were defective. But they were all mine. There are dust-bag expert witnesses, mind you, on this litigious earth, and shelves of dust-bag literature we had the clerks going through.

And the gym was sending reams of treadmill cases, the conveyers gobbling up people's Nikes and sending them back as rubber and canvas pancakes. Some had taken toes, and one a whole foot. In her opening statement a plaintiff's lawyer had struck her theme: "This is the story of a hungry machine."

George was my soul mate, the guy I started with at the firm, and he sat now in the next office with Mr. Bad News. Bad News was my client, and George was helping me out. Bad News was an aging process server and all-purpose enforcer. Lately he'd been posting foreclosure notices. Whatever he did, people got hurt. He went to the wrong house. He stepped on things.

Bad News's voice was loud, metallic like a bullhorn. I didn't want to go in to George's office to see him because then they'd think I really hadn't been that busy. But I didn't want to not go in either, because the two might walk by and see me sitting there. I put my listening glass against the wall.

"So I'm right at the door with the lady, right, and I'm pushing in the screen."

"Right," said George.

"Right at the door, at the screen right? And she's up in my face at the screen, right? And she tells me I got the wrong place, right? 'You'se got the wrong house,' she says, right?"

"Gotcha. She's trying to throw you off."

"She's dodging, she's dodging is what she's doing. I had enough to sign the affidavit right there."

Mr. Bad News is rapping on his papers, just as he always does, with the back of his knuckles.

"So why didn't you; why'd you go through the screen?"

"I thought I had access. That screen was tore."

"You practically knocked her into next week! She's got a lien chiropractor on it already."

Bad News was a man of ominous silences. I knew he was standing there—sitting there—with George, just as he always did with me when I nailed him. He needed an out to get him started again.

"And she landed on her grandma's teak end table." George was learning. "Crushed it to bits."

"That chifforobe? The bag *fell* on it."

"Fifteen K, the appraiser says."

"I seen better at Value Village."

"Zeke," said George, closing his pad, "It's always one damn thing or another. Why don't you put it in their hands and leave?"

Bad News cleared his throat. "Because people evade. People stay hid. I seen people go down under their desks."

"It has to be fair, Zeke. Constitutionally legit. And it *can't* be when you're leaving them black and blue."

Another silence started—Bad News slumped in his chair. Then, very softly—I could hear the arms squeaking—he was getting back up again, and George along with him.

"Did she *come* at you with something?" George started working it. "Did she pull back that screen door and slam it in your face?"

Bad News was thinking because I could hear him humming. Just as he stared to say, "Now that you mention it . . ." I heard their door open, and they were walking my way.

I got up and pushed mine shut, but not before Bari's red figure strode by. Her body was a whirlwind of red dust and flame. Her eyes glowed green-pink, like great Biblical worms. Her dress was some sort of thin black tickweave—a burlap shift that made me think of monkhood and bells.

≳

I looked down at my workload to restabilize. The Tabonga file was the one that jumped up at me: another family victim of the Tongan-Samoan wars. Tonga's exiled monarch, King Freddy, had set up in San Jose with an emaciated militia and his old cabinet and staff. The Samoan King Amos had moved there as well. Lately, in the heat-blazed hills of Silicon Valley, they'd warred over their claims to some old fly-specked islands. It was providing a lot of work for the coroner and us.

Freddy's boys had Mausers in their sandbagged duplex and bulletproof stretch limos that spewed out leaden rain. Amos went for gang attacks—drugged, stabbing teens. My client's daughter had gotten caught in one of Freddy's firefights. When I sat with her mother looking at her snapshots, I practically gasped at her animal beauty. Did I imagine that nimbus around her head, that wiry Gauguin island child's halo?

The first snap in the file showed the angel under sheets, a giant widening spot of blood around her head. Somebody had dropped a lighter by her toes, and it lay there horribly in the flashbulb's light, which caught each tiny thing's scatteredness and guilt—the stupidity and melancholy of every object.

There was a knock at the door, George's one hangdog thunk. He came in holding up a lottery card.

"I dream of it every day," he said. "I guess it's come to this."

He turned the thing over to the instruction side, sliding it slowly along the bristles of his beard. The way his beard joined his hair made him look Melvillean—the little windswept circles and sprinkles of gray.

"I mean, I can *see* myself walking up to that plastic thing of revolving balls and *claiming* my big prize money."

His voice had the ring of a joke in it but also the ring of the definitely crazed. His eyes were frenetic, exhausted, and pink.

I said, kidding, "Would you keep working?"

He looked at me, trying to think of a line.

"*Tread marks* outside my office, I'd be out of here so fast," I said.

"Ditto to that."

"Gone, man," I said, lifting my glass. This is how the

two of us toasted every day: to being the gone men, to being away.

"The bitch was complaining about spots on her rims."

There were two of these kids, each yapping in my ear, both on the same phone and taking turns. But it wasn't like either of them *wanted* to talk. Epping, their boss, had to practically threaten them, which made me wonder why he hadn't fired them first.

"The bitch's got major attitudinal problems." This was Tim speaking, the tall one, I knew, from the probation photo Kiley had taped to my desk. His hair stuck out in big rooster shocks. He was saying this more for his co-worker, Bobby, than for me or for any truth it contained. Kiley had Bobby's picture taped there too—a squat, pasty face with watery eyes and a wide, rotten smile with numbers underneath.

"Spots on her rims?" said Bobby. "We'd never done that."

"No way," said Tim. "We got a policy, a specified policy against spots on the rims."

"What did you do when she started complaining? I hope not what it says here in the complaint."

"Those *aller*gations? What do they say?" He was bright enough, I could tell from the sound of his voice, to be deliberately mispronouncing the word. He laughed nervously and passed the phone over to Bobby.

When the facts are really bad, a smart client can tell, and eventually they'll start coming in short of the truth. It's not the best idea, but they do it, and sometimes you find yourself cueing them along. But these guys were intoxicated with whatever had happened; their minds were up roaring on a whole other level.

"The woman was complaining."

"*Fucking* complaining."

"Up in our fucking *faces* complaining."

"But you didn't, I mean . . . what did you do after that?" My palms were sweating now. I kept shifting the phone.

"She was in there."

"In where?"

"In the oven."

"How in the, let me ask how . . ."

". . . she got in there?" Bobby, this Bobby, finishing my sentences. "She said she wanted to go in and look. Said it looked like the paint might be uneven."

"But you were never supposed to let a customer in the kiln."

"She *wanted* to be in there. She *made* us let her in."

"Who turned the kiln on? Tim, tell me who."

"It was an accident." Now we were rolling. I was almost believing him, his accentless voice.

"There's two kilns. I thought we were switching on the other."

"Are the switches together? Was there a car in the other one? Does the log have a car marked down in the other?"

"Yeah, we marked another car in the log."

More voices and then scuffling, a scraping on the desk. The longer the silence and its scratchy undersounds, the more I knew Tim would be the one I needed—the memory, the talker, the other car logger. He would be the one with the answers we'd need.

"You didn't *tell* her to go in, did you?"

The scraping got louder, then a loud metal squeak.

"Tim, what did you—"

"We turned it off."

"What did you tell her?"

"We turned the thing off, man. What do you want? We turned the thing off when she started to scream."

I was driving to the site with the address taped to the dash: 1430 Hardin, corner Hardin and Normandie. Everything looked fine through most of the South Side, but I started seeing burned blocks not far past the USC campus. It was a week or two after the L.A. riots, mid-May, the city still hissing and flickering cinders. For long stretches everything looked perfectly normal—huge parking lots and facades of pastel—but then the burned smell would come back to my nostrils, and mounds of black lumber and brick would loom up.

Naturally, the thought of fire got me thinking of her. I saw her out in front of me, like a Thanksgiving float. Bari, dead center on Normandie Avenue! With her breasts and the points of her chopped, swaying hair.

When I turned on to Hardin, things started looking worse. Nothing had been burned, but there was still the singed smell. The street was full of beat-up sofas and chairs and lamps and water coolers and bent hat stands. If these things weren't fallen over with holes kicked in their sides, it would've been like anybody could have walked up and used them, as if there were people down here who were living outside.

Looking at all this made you realize where you were— the kind of place where people only ended up, where you'd only be found if horrors pressed down on you. The focus of everything was a little bit off, so the background loomed hugely and made everything grow small. Mattresses burned in the street, and around them was broken furniture in tiny colored piles.

I guessed it was Bobby who answered the plate door. His face was yellow and very concave—most probably from a lifetime of being punched—and it had a lot of the kind of pockmarks on it that made it look as though someone had held him down and beat it, repeatedly, with a bag of coins.

Tim too had a face like a banana, one with its skin just spotting with brown. His head was even longer and more bent than Bobby's. Their nails and hair were long, and it seemed intended to match their colorful Iron Maiden T-shirts. I'd read that our cells could do these kinds of things after we died and were put in our coffins, the nails and hair continuing to grow. Tim had a silver ring in his nose. I'd never seen that on a man.

"Hey, lawyer." Bobby said.

"Hey what?"

"*Hey* is *hi*," said Tim. "It's the same as *hi* where we come from."

"The South," said Bobby. "Atlanta, Gee-Aye."

"What part?" I asked, trying to make conversation.

"You're familiar?"

"No," I said. The two of them looked at each other. Bobby wheezed like a small machine when he breathed.

This office of theirs was divided from the kilns and the spraying floor by a big one-way window. Through it, you could see the last few employees working the spray guns, which were connected to the ceiling with thick, drooping hoses.

"Make sure Gum-Gum checks *himself* out," said Tim.

"Check," said Bobby.

"No funny business," said Tim.

"No funny business."

"I'll do funny business on his head again if Rud checks him out like last time," said Tim.

"That was quite a number you did on him," said Bobby. "I didn't know that many stitches could fit on a face."

They both broke into a laugh. Bobby's laugh ended with the same slow wheezes as when he breathed.

After a minute and their noticing I wasn't laughing, Tim said, "I suppose you want to look at the log."

"That'd be great," I said.

"You sit here," said Tim. "I'll get it."

"I'll stay here with you," said Bobby. He sat down on one of the broken chairs and watched me. He was smiling. It was more of a leer, the kind men give women in bars, but with a colder, blanker light behind it. In fact, his eyes looked empty. They were zeroes.

I could hear the same clamping and clomping I'd heard over the phone earlier coming from the next room where Tim was. Then, to the left of me, somebody was rapping on the one-way window. When I peered close, I could see it was the last employee—Gum-Gum, I guessed—waving his time card at Bobby. I was glad the glass was a little blurred because I didn't want to see Gum-Gum's face. Bobby waved him away.

I took a file out of my briefcase and pretended to be

looking at it. Bobby sat there with one elbow on his knee, and his wheezing breathing started to get stronger until it seemed like he was almost gasping for breath. But I should have guessed; he was asthmatic. He took one of those little inhaler things out of a Marlboro pack and started working it with his thumb.

All around us, on the long table the two of us sat at each end of, there were little square pocket mirrors and pages ripped out of magazines. It made the place look glittery and cheap, like the windows of Indian sari shops I'd seen up on Melrose.

"I guess Lawyer can come on in here," said Tim. "Seeing's how you and I talked earlier."

Bobby was still spraying his inhaler but waved me on in.

Tim sat with the logbook open in his hands. There were two file cabinets next to the stool he sat on and a steel desk by the door that I eased myself onto. One file cabinet had several drawers open, and in the shadows of one I could see the big checkered grip of a revolver.

I took the index card with all the jobs I'd been able to find out about and started checking it against the log. Before I got too far down, Tim said, "It's there."

When I got down to the names and plate numbers for the right hour, I could see a second car hadn't really been logged. Actually, one *had* been logged, but it was one we'd verified had left a lot earlier.

"This car wasn't in there then. They're going to say there was no reason for you going for the switches when you did."

Tim looked over at Bobby.

The most important of client moments (Kiley's quote) had come: "I'm not the enemy," I said. "I'm with you guys. You just got to tell me what happened."

"We thought we could trust you with some things," Tim went on. "We thought we'd let you in on some. Being our lawyer, it'd stay with you."

Tim's eyes narrowed when he looked at me but widened when he looked over my shoulder at Bobby. For a second I wanted to ask what was going on. But of course, what was going on was the last thing I wanted to know. Things were getting so disconnected now, I just wanted to make sure there was nothing I could do for these guys, that I could just cut them loose and substitute out.

They must have sensed the fear in me too, because Tim balked. The two of them went back to keeping me in the dark.

"What happened," said Bobby, "is what we said."

The phone rang right then.

"It's probably Gum-Gum's wife," said Tim. Bobby

went back to the long, mirror-filled table in the big room to take it.

Tim seemed a lot less talkative then. He eased the file drawer all the way shut, and when I offered the logbook back to him he shook his head.

Looking up, I could see the light was on in the nearest kiln, the one she had been in. It was a low, ghastly kind of cold light, the kind that comes from florescent bulbs. I went up to the window and looked in. There were handprints all along the wall that I thought had been made from her touching some kind of paint. It took a second and some of the smell coming in through the window crack before I knew they were made out of her skin, her actual flesh.

Bobby had been shouting into the phone, and now he was in the doorway shouting.

"It was O-lan," he said, breathless. "Federal agents, she's pretty sure."

Tim put his feet on the floor, but not before his one foot pulled the drawer back out and Bobby lifted up the gun. There was another one under that, an automatic, that he handed to Tim.

"Where are the fucking shells?" asked Tim, and Bobby pulled out a fanny pack that read, YOU PARK IT, WE'LL PAINT IT. He emptied the clips into Tim's palm.

Then they started opening the other drawers. Was that the point I first heard the siren? I couldn't really tell, because it seemed at first like the sound was in my head. It might have been, I thought, the one I manufactured a lot lately, the little cry Bari made in the dark of her bed.

But then there were more and they were closer. They were real.

"Lawyer," said Tim, "you better get gone." They were loading bags of white powder with Spanish words stenciled in blue into an empty cardboard box that had held paper towels. There was a second door from this small room, one leading away from the kiln and into a garage, where a car was waiting.

The street outside now was filled with revolving blue and red electric light. The lights came in through the windows and moved through our hair.

Bobby and Tim were almost out the door by then. But I was pretty much frozen there by the desk. Have you ever woken up and wondered how your life had gotten to the point where it could put you in the place you were? It's like that Talking Heads song about the beautiful wife and the beautiful house, the one that goes, "How did I get here?" If all other things had been normal, I would have said it was just my being nutty with grief over Bari, but there were so many other little points of desolation: the stupid social pressures of the firm, insistent and sinister, and the mounds of files I couldn't see the end of. And other, deeper things: the traffic, the static on the radio, the insomnia I'd had all winter, and the ghostly noise I'd begun to hear under me in the pillows when I tossed and turned each night, beating out a shape for my loneliness.

I could hear the officers out beyond the plate door of the other room. At first they banged it with their shoes and pistol butts. When that didn't work, they started to slam against it, in a slow, steadily rising rhythm, with the broad steel stocks of their bigger guns.

GETTING HECTOR

And when they went to bring back the body of Hector, there was sorrow upon the land, sorrow like a river; sorrow to which no further sorrow could be added.

HOMER, *Iliad*

I KNOW the kid we're going in to get. I mean I went to school with him, Tom Margavich. He was one of those kids whose awkward lankiness always left him fighting his own body, pulling moves that looked as if he were jerking himself awake or stopping himself in the middle of his long, long, almost-adult-size stride. You could tell he hated his nose, the great hook of it, the way it glistened.

And he would never, ever look you in the eyes, so when long hair came in and the mop of it could cover his eyes and the top of his inimitable schnoz, he was happy. He was quieter, less fidgety.

His people were different: Hungarians, factory workers, something. The men didn't hunt, or so my father said. Once at a wedding the women wore native costumes, blazing white blouses bright as neon, with blue Magyar shifts stitched up in black, tilting crosses. I saw it. It was like they were covered with a language, a whole alphabet of rolling *X*'s.

People think that when somebody commits suicide and the police come in and take their report and such that they just stick around and clean up any mess the guy might have made. That's not the way it works. If there's no cleaning to be done, if it was pills or gas, the family makes the same arrangements with the funeral home they'd make if it had been a natural death.

But if there are blood and brains and bone chips on the walls and carpet, or if somebody's been found after a long time and the scene is septicemic, that's where we come in. No one else can do it, as a matter of state law. We're licensed by the Department of Toxic Substances Control, and for anybody but ourselves to clean the plate is a felony.

If you can handle it, the money is tremendous. After

a couple of years and up to the burn-out point, you can sock away a lot of money. Then the trick is to hand it off to a colleague or a friend. A strong, strong-stomached friend. A friend who's seen some things, who can take in whole worlds of pain as though it were a glass of cold water he was downing.

Most of the snuffs we see now are druggies, people who've been through rehab the normal three or four times, at enormous expense, until the insurance runs out and their families have ejected them from the house or garage, and the county has stopped them from sleeping in the public parks. It isn't just meth, though that is a lot of what we see up in the rural counties around Wooster and Ashland, where there's little other than Amish and race-tracks. Meth is covered heavily now because it provides the best pictures for the news magazines, which, like CNN, all seem to be going the way of *Entertainment Tonight*. *Time* and *Newsweek* and local Region sections of the Cleveland papers love pictures of emaciated twenty-year-olds look-ing like Appalachian women in old sharecropper photo-graphs, the close-ups of rotting teeth and gums and open sores, the flesh's rapid giving way, the holes in the sides of cheeks that users can run their tongues through.

But there's a lot of crack too, which sounds like *crank* in the hook that it has, the way it lassoes the whole neu-ronal system, ties it up.

I imagine it as some kind of spirit, a genie setting itself up inside your bones.

On the morning Cruikshank and I have to get Margavich, Fergus has us sitting in front of his desk full of toxics trades and price sheets and Notre Dame memorabilia. Cruik sits with the tips of his fingers joined. He fancies himself a world-class badass and loves the fact his nickname sounds like *crook*. But I see him as a possible lifer on this gig. Fergus tries to appear as though he were the CEO of a serious scientific company but rarely comes off as looking anything more than pathetic. He talks about the Fighting Irish constantly, calls it his school. But I know the closest he ever got to it was seeing its steeples above the trees when he drove by on the Indiana Turnpike. Somehow he's heard Tom was an old school friend of ours, and he wants to break it to us that it's going to be a particularly hard job without telling us exactly why.

"Know you guys knew him," he says. He is rolling up a Bugler and won't look away from the tamping motion he makes with his fingers. The blotches on his face could be wine stains, melanoma, anything. With every twist of his fingers, his glasses slide further down his nose until they stop at the red bumps of broken veins. "Lets you know lesson number one in life. Which is, it don't pay to love. World's going to break your heart sooner or later."

We've heard the speech a couple times before. He'd given it to us when we had to get his duck hunting partner Chet Hurlihey, who'd eaten his Walther after his wife threw him out of their trailer and he was living with Brownie at the old man's shack at the dump. Fergus, when ramping up the world-breaking-heart thing, always brings in the Kennedy assassination. "Man was going about his business, just trying to get on the freeway," he says. "Man was just waving to the people along the roadside." He tries to make his voice sound like it's breaking, but you can tell he's ginning it up. "Ever think how hard," he says, rubbing one eye, "it is to be president?"

Fergus gave us the same sob job when we had to get Johnny Vanderbilt's boy after he'd hung himself in the barn. The kid had only wrecked the family truck, something that stupid. But the sheriff found him with his neck slack as a towel, a mini step ladder kicked away in the straw. By the time we got there, he'd been cut down and laid on a gurney without wheels, just an army stretcher. He wore bibs and a long-sleeved Eddie Bauer camo T-shirt. What Fergus saw was something similar to the young president, all that promise wasted. But the boss was nowheres near the kid. He was on the walkie-talkie to us, and when he started in with the Lancelot crap we turned down the volume and worked there by ourselves in silence, in the clammy barn dark.

"It was a long time ago we knew Margavich," Cruikshank says. "It was the sixties. Sixth grade." I remember seeing Margo in line in the cafeteria, the only kid whose parents let him wear patterned pants, bell-bottoms. *Disraeli Gears* had just come out. Another thing I remember about him was the way he held one hand in front of his eye sometimes. It was like somebody taking one of those vision tests, following the doctor's instructions. Later, it looked to me like the guy in Michelangelo's painting sitting with his hand like that in the boat, getting whipped by the devil, who looked like Yoda.

"Still," says Fergus. He looks at his shelves of graybound trade rags, easing the Bugler pouch back in his pocket. "The promise." I sigh just enough to let him know we think little promise lost with Margo other than maybe some explosion burns and missing fingers, a little time at the Lima Honor Farm.

I look over at Cruik, who you can tell is anxious to suit up. The yellow hazmat suit is over his shoulder, lying like a giant wilted jungle leaf. Cruik's suit is unusually slim fitting, almost like the purple bowling outfit of the John Turturro pervert in *The Big Lebowski*. Mine feels as roomy as a circus tent. "Cyndie likes the way it looks on me," he says.

"There's a little hosey space for my dick, like the Michelin Man's."

Fergus starts to get up, faking his bad back, and is about to leave us with his usual parting, "See you girls later," when a stack of dog-eared trades knocks the burning butt out of the ashtray and onto his lap. "Bosom of goddamn *Mary*," he says, slapping the coals away and dousing them with a splash of Dr. Pepper. Walking out the door, we hear the hesitation in his voice, the feeling he had something else to tell us. But what could it be? Another day, another first job body. But one we'd stood in line with when Nixon was president, waiting for our wiener winks and apple crisp.

We suit up in the head, which is agency rated and has gunmetal gray toilets and shower walls covered with disposable plastic liners. The hazmat suits look heavy, but they're actually comfortable. And cool: The compressed air from the ventilator tank works like a scuba getup, giving you air to breathe and filtering the same cold whoosh of oxygen out of little jets in the armpits and waist and down in the booties.

The first hazmat job we had was another one of Fergus's "Johnny We Hardly Knew Ye" episodes, and it was a gig that taught us that when in doubt, you put on the rubber.

He was one of Fergus's doctors, or a doctor friend of one of his doctors. The scene was like what I'd read about in Hemingway bios, right down to the guy being in electro-shock therapy and unable to work or screw adequately in his last few months. He'd put both barrels of a twelve-gauge against the palate and tripped each trigger with separate toes, so the whole cranial vault had lifted off and the top skull quadrant was sunk an inch or two into the ceiling plaster.

We didn't see any liquid tissue going in, nothing wet enough to go in the pores of our skin. I almost backed out and unsuited. But then we saw it: brains dripping in a corner over an open window. All the blood was dried, but the gray stuff stayed movable from the moisture blowing in. It was a sweet, late spring day. Fluids from a body can be poisonous as hell. There are acids in the liver and kidneys, the stomach. In a few days they've got the power of strychnine or cyanide, once they combine with the air. A drop of that shit on Cruik's head would have opened a space as big as a bullet hole. It might have taken a few hours, but it would happen.

We found out later that the guy was a Demerol addict, like a lot of doctors. The combination of the medicine with the bodily fluids, it turns out, made the tissue even more dangerous to be around. It seemed sad to be piecing somebody together and at the same time pushing them back in a way, refusing to touch them.

≋

Booties were important too. One crankhead couldn't shake his habit, couldn't toss the back monkey. They'd tried everything: meetings, isolation rehab, even a pure chemical cure, where they Keith Richards your blood through some kind of filtration system. He'd slit himself, quite effectively, lengthwise, with a razor. Cruik almost stepped on that, though it probably wouldn't have gone through his Kevlar soles.

But there was something else with that guy. He'd been in there awhile, a good three or four days. Flies had gotten all over him. They'd laid their eggs, and some had hatched into maggots, which made for more and more flies. But some of the eggs hadn't hatched when the sun hit the room and heated it up enough to kill the larvae inside. They just dried and turned into husks, little brittle trails that would have been invisible except for their sound. As you came in around the bed you could hear the *skush*, *skush*, *skush* of your own footsteps. It was like walking through boxes of spilled Rice Krispies, or listening to the hiss and rustle of a stiff-hemmed dress.

≋

Sound. It's a big part of the job, the tunes I put on my iPod and zipper up inside the front pouch of my suit. Since you never know what you're going to find (maxim numero uno), you want premium optimistic materials coming through your earphones when you're driving out. Radiohead is too dark and layered, but Arcade Fire is peppy with all the crescendoing strings and the singer's edgy, David Byrne–like voice. The song with the lyric "Don't want to work in a building downtown" is like a case of Red Bull straight into the carotid. You feel powerful enough to stand up right through the roof of the King Cab.

But the time I needed calming most, when I was about ready to flip my shit, I clicked on Death Cab for Cutie—those foggy, pine-scented, tranquil ballads like "Your Heart Is an Empty Room" and "Transatlanticism." The guy we were cleaning had been in his bed for two months. He weighed 570 pounds.

Mr. Finakal taught us in biology how much of the body is water. You see how true that is with decomposition, and with a massive cadaver the liquid content is truly enormous. Even in a hot room Flipper (Cruik named him that) had shrunk by two-thirds, and his body was under a square pool, formed by the bed frame, of the water and fluids hardening into a kind of translucent gel. When we turned on the suction the sheet of liquid just kind of wavered over him, rocking gently like lake water. But when the draining got so powerful it pulled pieces of flesh off his face, the chunks of it lifting loose and spinning, a cold cloud came into my head. My knees started to give. And that's when I turned the music on, smelling salts to a fainting man: the breezy chord progressions of "Bixby Canyon Bridge," the trumpets and harps in "Marching Bands of Manhattan." I have to say it saved me. In fact, it helped me concentrate. I felt something like a musician myself.

We're driving out to get Margo. Cruik driving, me going over the job sheets. I know it's a suicide and a meth call, and I'm hoping there hasn't been a lot of fire, the walls charred and the body burned. We have contracts with a lot of motels to clean up after tweakers, people who rent a room to cook up meth. A night of that work can lead to a fire or somebody just sampling until their heart goes out: *pow*, arrhythmia. And the collateral cleanup is nasty: fifty or sixty pounds of clean meth generates about five hundred pounds of waste. And all of it smells awful, like jet fuel, like the fumes that come in your window when you drive by a refinery.

My first meth job had me hitting the music hard, closing my eyes and just following the sound along to keep from vomiting. The orange and yellow residue was all over the walls, and phosphorous embers had fallen into the cheap carpeting and burned its surface back into a blackish plastic.

But the guy, he was something to see. Half of him was intact: We were there forty-eight to seventy-two hours post episode. But the side that faced the explosion—he must've just lay down when it blew—was something like you see in a Chinatown window. There is nothing worse than burned flesh. It's more like barbecue meat than anything else. Only half of him burned because the flames were stopped by his spinal fluid and brain exploding, foaming everywhere to the left of the left eye and nostril.

Goya couldn't have painted this shit. He couldn't have seen it in all his wars. The kid's left set of ribs arched up blackly like a fireplace grate. It was as though somebody had opened a piano, trying to see the places where the hammers met the strings.

≈

I watch the landscape, wondering why I'm not more numbed by this job. It's a kind of war, really, and I remember the stories of tank gunners north of Baghdad, watching the road and waiting for IEDs at any second, how they keep the phones on and the tunes flowing—thinking and not thinking, waiting for anything, absolutely anything, to happen.

I look over at Cruik and wonder what's on his mind, how long he's signed up for all this. He looks pasty, the color of his skin running, the same crumpled wet as the paper towels in a gas station bathroom. The rain-ready sky up behind his window the same gray. He blends right into it.

The color, the vividness of my life now, I realize it's all in the work. Orange and yellow powders, exploded things, the brightness of fresh blood. Everything that gives you awe, that makes your mouth drop open and look and look again: It's all in things that blast and blow away. The normal things? The world you measure all that hellacious crap against, that gives most people peace? The shine had gone out of all of it. *The bright and faded bartered, traded places.* It's like a Neil Young line, or maybe Milton. Heaven and hell get switched around.

We come up the drive where Margo has lived the last few months, one of those apartments in a giant, greenish wooden block of them that dentists and bankers build for people who'd never buy here, who are waiting, like everybody, to get out to somewhere else. We park the truck and finish zipping. We have computer-generated body location maps and go back the long hallway where the Sharpied blue arrows point, and damned if the hallway isn't blue too, light robin's-egg blue as clear as a cloudless Great Lakes sky. No scorches, no fires. At least not here. I've got the Talking Heads' "Houses in Motion" on the Pod, actually a tension builder with its Moroccan drums and queasy insect buzzing, a good number to get you moving toward a thing you'd rather just not face.

And there it is through the open bedroom door, a right leg stretched out with a bright green ski sock flopped over on his toe, like a Smurf's hat. Margo never had much fashion sense—those paisley-print pants back in grade school were actually god-awful. Same with the Magyar dirndls of his womenfolk.

Cruik springs into action, entering the room first and moving over to the far side of the bed where the exit wound would be if it were a right-hand shot. I motion Cruik to stand down, going up to where Margo's fingers were curled around the trigger before the cops lifted the pistol away. What remains of his face is in the shadow of the drapes, and I see he's got a beard like the Amish grow in these parts, thick only along the jawline and the upper chin, the lip clean-shaven.

⇌

There's a shaft of light coming through the parted drapes. Cruik is antsy, wants to move. With one hand I gesture no,

and with my other hand I pull up a chair and sit, waiting
for the light to move.

In ten minutes the sun hits the right side of the pillow. Another pillow on top of that has blocked the exit
spray. Cruik won't have much work, and I see him calming
down, grateful there won't be a lot of someone we knew
to work on.

The beam moves slowly, slowly, like a sundial. It spreads
over his face, the big ridge of his nose, and that's when I see
it: the hand over the eye. Cupped just like he used to.

Cruik moves back, and the hose of the enzyme vacuum spreads the curtain wider, the shaft of sun moving
over the bed straight toward me. It lands on my chest, a
pillar of light pouring straight into my heart.

The tears drop down and click on my goggle bottoms,
and they steam, and I lift them and wipe the insides with
a pillowcase, knowing it's safe. Cruik's head falls forward,
refusing to look at me. He doesn't like emotion.

*This is the way the world ends. This is the way the world
ends* for Margo. Not with a whimper, but with a goddamn
Walther PPK/S. In three weeks we'll have the first high
school reunion I'll go to. He's the eighth to go this way.
Maybe there will be a set of candles.

But then I notice something, something the opposite
of what I expect just now that I'm losing it. The sunlight

shows the room to be decently put together. Tidy, in fact. And more than that: The bedspread, untouched by any blood at all, has the faintest glimmer down in the stitches of its cloth, a sparkle. The pattern is of green and silver elephants on some Hindu heaven river, moving through whitish grasses and wearing etched and checkered saddles—yellow and purple and umber and aquamarine. Only Margo's body is dark.

The bedspread colors aren't exactly jumping out. They aren't like the scarves and spices in the Italian market in Youngstown. But there's something there that wasn't there before. The sunbeam moves across the caravan design like firelight on the cave walls we read about with Finakel. God, it is something. The elephants move so slowly with it, the carpets and flowers strapped to their broad, gray, rocking backs.

It makes me back up and think, not think but *see*, the rest of the picture that holds the guy, the Margo guy with his hand on his face in his coffin boat—the whole broad vault of the painted chapel ceiling. I remember the rest of it, the swirling robes, the angels wrapped in their girdles of stars. The old bearded man reaching down to Adam. Their fingers touching, the fire passing between them that started everything.

THE WAY IT CAME

BUDDY HOFFENBACH had never really seen a deer outside of the woods before, like this one now in the middle of the road looking right down the white line at him, the legs that had lifted it clumsily up there only seconds before now as stiff as a statue's, its eyes burning pink. He'd seen them, of course, from the stands his older brothers had shot them from and carried them back to, places where he could never get his rifle out of the scabbard fast enough—the tail wagging away from him like a mocking flag unless Darrell or Goines was able to cover it and bring it down.

But this one was just there, not running but standing still like a picture out in front of the windshield, like one of

Althea's porcelain figurines plucked out of some heavenly cabinet and laid down there by God. As his foot shifted to the brake, the animal lifted its head slightly, and above the nervous rabbit's motion of the nose he saw the rack: a good ten or twelve points, maybe fifteen. Bigger than any he'd seen on any of his family's walls.

This was where things began to slow, to drag, as if the world had been wound down by some horrible camera or plunged underwater. It wasn't his actual movements or the deer's that slowed, but the way he saw them, as if his eyes and nerves were the waterlogged things, so that he was inside the whole harsh screech and clatter of the crash, *fastened* to it, before he could have avoided the animal, avoided slamming the brake, avoided what he seemed joined to by something or someone working up behind it all in the gray, cold, backcountry sky.

It was like the descriptions of crashes he'd seen on television for years: the big, brown, now human-feeling body passing up over the grill of the Fairlane—the seconds of pain ticking high in his chest—and the hard parts of the body, the hooves and great basketlike thicket of antlers and eyes and now foam-lathered mouth all floating up over the slanted glass and roof and back into the black and brakelight-pinkened air, dropping with what he thought would be a thud but was already so distant that it sounded soft, like the tap of a woman's slipper against a wood floor.

And there it was now in his rearview mirror, stiller even than it had been in the instant he hit it.

Once the noise of the brakes and its echo was gone, there was no sound inside the car where he sat with his eyes open. Nothing: perfectly silent. And then the beating of his heart, loudening in the dark sparkle of the trees, and the tiniest hiss of steam from the radiator.

And then a ticking, a dieseling in the engine.

When even these sounds had stopped, Buddy thanked God quickly for getting him through it all unscathed. These prayers were like all the other ones he'd ever uttered: necessary but quick, one or two ladder steps that lifted him to a place his curiosity could look out from and work on. "Amen," he said, his hands not meeting, but almost joined from the way his big arms lay heavy with relief on the wheel.

He looked back. A big buck, maybe a trophy, dead in the middle of the road. It was the only one he'd ever killed, something, again like so many other things, set down and arranged for him, put there to make him sigh and shake his head sadly at his sad luck. It seemed to have come out of a script, right down to the exaggerated hunch of his arms on the fur cover of the wheel and the way the prayer had spurted out of him, like a cry of pain.

Buddy wondered whether this praying, this sense of fate that he took with Althea to Reverend Chapin's congregation every Sunday, was what kept him so far behind his brothers, stumbling and wheezing constantly to catch up with them. Goines's wife, Janet, still went to church, and though Darrell's wife, Bev, had gone in the earlier years before her faith had tapered off with the death of their son, she still seemed the kind that would go if she could muster it. But neither of the brothers were church-going men as he was. They seemed the opposite: the kind that didn't need church; the kind whose brittle eyes and attitudes and plans put them so in control of the world, so in command, that offers of guidance would do nothing but slow them, drag down their stride.

~

From where he stood now, searching for the carcass in the moonlit, cindered road, an idea rose in Buddy's brain like bubbles popping on the surface of a pool: certain, clear, involuntary, and designed (made up, of themselves) to leave no trace. He was surprised at how quickly the notion came to him, given how the painkillers had slowed his reaction to so many things, making one thought follow another faithfully but slowly, like his road crew boots moving through the thick snow of a new morning. After his accident with the shovel, when the workmen's comp doctor had noticed him asking for higher doses of Oxy, he'd gotten worried even before the German shrink's first warnings about dependency. Why, after all, had this stuff been in the papers so much? And what if he took one on a day when he wasn't really hurting? What if he took a whole pill instead of just a quarter?

But he was at a new, high, open place with this medicine. The sweet, sweet heat-coil rise and bloom of it, the blanketing warmth, the calm that came into his temples and thickening back and palms—all of it was so relieving, so forgiving, so *right*. And it was all so much cleaner, more dignified than the beer and Seagram's their father had plunged himself under for years. This stuff might suck you in, Buddy thought, like so many other men's poisons. But he felt himself to be always passing through its doors with a kind of neatness, a trim speed the rest of his life didn't always have. There was no crying like there was with booze, no smell. There was no falling down.

He looked down at the great brown and white body of the buck. The impact hadn't opened its hide at all. He would take it back and wait for Althea to go to her nursing shift and then lay it out in the yard and fire a shot through its neck with his .30-30. One clean kill on a rack that large: What could his two almighty brothers really say to that?

There would be no rolling of the eyes as he'd seen from Darrell when the two older men had inspected his woodworking, sizing up his guesthouse joists as they circled him with their hands in their pockets. Carpentry came as easily to them as everything else, especially so since their father was a finish carpenter of no small talent. Darrell hadn't laughed, but the zigzag saw scars and bent nail marks were something Buddy knew Darrell would pocket and talk about with Goines once they were alone, over whiskey, on an antelope hunt he wouldn't be invited to. He imagined Darrell's face now, looking at the buck hanging down from those same rafters. He could see the man's wide, dumb mouth drop and his hooked eyes rise, counting the points until there were so many he would give up.

But Goines would be even more dumbfounded. Yes, Goines would be truly amazed. He was the more detached, icier one, looking down even on Darrell sometimes as much as on him. After all, both Darrell and Buddy worked with their hands, made their living with them, while Goines wore crisp ties and polished shoes to work. Goines had standards neither brother could meet, standards very few people in the world could even come close to—not his wife, not his kids, certainly not the men under him on his sales force. Where did he get that *drive*, Buddy wondered, that arm-pumping thunder that sped him along like a tank that could roll over anything. The cuts that Goines made at Buddy— almost all related to building and hunting—would boil up out of the older brother like an acid, their fumes standing like smoke behind the moisture of his metal glasses. But what in the world could he say to this buck? There would be no challenging this giant, overdue trophy.

Buddy backed the car up until the taillights fell over the long, bent, blood-speckled lump. The white of its neck and tail were clean, and the white of its belly, the white of its hooves. His bumper had caught it just behind the bent rack, breaking the shoulder bone which swelled now in a darkened hematoma.

Perfect was the word going through his mind as he lifted the door latch. The shoulder was where he'd fire the shots, not the neck; the swelling would then look perfectly natural. Both brothers had always told him it was the ideal kill point.

The trunk was filled with cinder bags. He looked in his trunk for a rope and found nothing, just as he expected he would. His brothers almost relished the idea of a flat, jacking and jumping, spinning the wheel nuts with irons as they squinted and laughed. Buddy's trunk contained nothing. He always called AAA.

He would have to put it in the backseat, something he'd heard done by some black hunters in Marshfield who bloodied their seats up and smelled their upholstery to kingdom come. It was the only thing he could do. He laid a drop cloth he'd bought for the guesthouse varnishing and never used across the backseat, tucking the corners of it down tightly in the folds.

The carcass was heavier than he expected. But when he thought about it, it seemed natural; the deer was almost as big as he was, maybe thirty or forty pounds less, 150 or 160. He'd never lifted that much. Who had?

He pulled it by the rack around to the driver's side of the Ford Fairlane. Once he got its head up into the doorway, and once its limp neck flopped over onto the seat, he crawled over it until he was in the middle and started pulling on the antlers again, taking deep breaths and throwing the whole weight of his body backward.

It must have taken him forty-five minutes to move the thing, inch by inch, to where he could climb out the other end and come around and push the last few inches of its rump in so the door would shut. Once it was closed, he brushed his hands together like people on TV when they had finished a chore.

Good job, he said to himself, still catching his breath. *Nobody's going to call me* fuckhead *anymore, not with this thing on the wall.* His side was beginning to ache, but he felt good. His shitbird days were definitely over.

The deer's weight gave good traction on the slick road. Cars were spinning out all over the highway in front of him. He would have stopped to help some of the women like he sometimes did, but he got the feeling that if the car came to a stop it would never get going again. The gold he carried was its own momentum. Besides, he was a good Samaritan enough of the time:

On the best nights of your life you had to be looking out for number one.

The night sky now was spitting snow: *tick, tick, tick, tick*, infinitesimal flakes that melted as soon as they landed. He was thinking of his gun in the closet, lying there unused for so long in its sheepskin case. He'd have to take the deer out to the gravel pit to get the shooting done. The noise would be too loud for the neighborhood. But he could do it. He'd tell Althea there'd been a call out for all the road crews to get a jump on the worsening snow.

Buddy looked up at the night sky, the dark edges of it ending in a foggy woods that lined the valley he headed into. The center of it, straight above him, looked so much lighter than usual, filled with a white or yellowish light that he'd expect to see approaching a city or on a warm spring night when trails of stars lay thick with light behind the haze. There was nothing now except this soft, unusual whiteness and the pale blue and orange glimmer of the dash dials and the radio, which he'd turned to country. Hank Williams's voice could make you sleepy, he knew, as it sometimes did when he was riding in the county truck, sometimes after a pill. But he was sure that wouldn't happen now. He'd taken some O, but he was wired, lit up like a bulb with what he'd found, with what he'd planned.

The first time the deer moved, it just lifted its head. The long neck came up very quickly and then stopped as its giant brown eyes fluttered. Buddy's heart felt warm and his sphincter tightened; he realized he hadn't taken care of that yet today.

When its head was back down it started making kicking sounds in the plastic, its hooves shaking frantically in the dropcloth.

Then, before Buddy could think another thought, it rose up and lunged backward until its rack slapped the rear window and sent up a puff of dust from the carpeting on the floor.

It made a sound, a horrible sound. A snort or a whining, something like he'd never heard.

What it had just done must have scared it plenty, because it was kicking all four feet now, the hooves that before had looked so small to him slamming against the seat like a bunch of baseball bats.

Then it calmed down. It lay back and breathed a deeper version of the whinny out through its nostrils, low and even, low and even, until it made a kind of rhythm with the tires crunching on the snowy road. Watching its brown belly swell and go down, Buddy had time to think what he'd thought before: *This isn't happening to me; this is what happens on* Rescue 911, *on* Real Stories of the Highway Patrol. But its breathing was real. Its rhythm and terrible sounds were real. The feel of the sweat on his temples was real.

The car skidded for a second, and he turned the wheel into the skid. In the rearview mirror, Buddy saw its eyes glow with fear at the shift in the car's direction, but even though it was still breathing, it had quieted, resting in the bloodied plastic. After a few minutes it was silent, and Buddy figured it was sleeping or passed out or had finally died.

Then the head came up again, rising higher than it had before, but with its eyes half open, covered with slime. They closed tighter as it lifted itself again and reared around, until one eye squirted a stream of fresh blood that fell back in a spray on the white of its face. It was giving out, Buddy knew, and for the first time he found himself wondering why he had waited so long to stop.

The last thing Buddy remembered was the flash of the antlers, a sound like plastic popping as his foot went onto the brake. The deer was facing the back window but whipping forward so fast the whole upper part of its body blurred. The first lunge went into the passenger side, the second halfway through Buddy's headrest. The third—it had moved down—sent two points through the back of his seat, one sinking into a kidney and the other sliding under his right shoulder blade.

His mouth filled with blood. He sneezed, and a fine red mist came out of his nose. Then darkness closed around him as he leaned forward on the wheel, his lips forming the first words of a prayer.

≈

The lights on the machines were the first things he could see, then the wires and tubes leading down from them to his bed; then, finally, the face of Althea with the worried smile and cracked forehead that he'd been tired of for so long but felt happy, so happy to see now. She didn't say anything, sitting there with her hand in his. Then she choked back a sob and let her face fall forward on his lap.

Buddy would still have been able to think none of this was really happening to him if it weren't for the pain. He could feel the two holes in the middle of his back, stinging and then numb, numb, and then burning, as if somebody had laid two fireplace coals on him there while he'd been sleeping on his stomach. His stomach: There was plenty of pain there too, the breathless kind that bends you double when you get it in the balls.

There were tubes inside his throat. The machine they came from blipped and jerked, pushing air down into his lungs.

He saw a young doctor come in and pick up the clipboard hanging on his bed frame. The man looked at Althea, her head still shaking, as if she were some kind of stranger who had wandered in to bother him and get in his way. An older doctor came in then and pointed to the chart, frowning and shaking his head and speaking sharply to the younger one. *Just my luck*, Buddy thought, *I get the pudnuts. I get horned by a deer, and I get the rookie doctor.*

His sight faded and came back in the pain and the drugs they gave him for it, the two working on each other like oil through the movements of an engine. Althea got up, the wetness still glimmering in her eyes. Behind her were doctors and technicians and what looked like janitors or mechanics bringing in plastic flowers and cups of medicine.

And then there was Darrell, and then Goines, coming out of the fog one right after the other. He couldn't believe it. He thought he was dreaming. He felt sure he was imagining Goines's spectacled eyes. But finally he smelled it: the smoke of one of Darrell's Luckies. Then he felt the older man's hand on his arm.

Goines's eyes were moist, like Althea's. It was the oddest thing Buddy had ever seen: the water in his middle brother's eyes, his nervousness, the high pitch his voice took on now. Buddy wasn't sure he liked this amount of feeling out of Goines. He'd only seen the man this moved about a fox he described stalking, or buying a new truck, or maybe a sale he'd just gotten a quote for. He lay back in the strange, surprising goodness of it all. It was like the unexpected warmth he felt roiling through the drug tubes: a deep, even heat pulsing through the center of the liquid cold.

He felt a slush in his chest, the presence of something, a container of fluid pressing on his ribs. It was Darrell who was talking, his big brother Darrell. Darrell, the mechanic, for whom everything worked. His loud voice was whispering, whispering *drainage,* whispering new things the doctors would try.

The face and the voice settled back in the mist, then came down in front of him, sharpening with form. He knew that his mind and his sight were wobbly; he decided to trust only what he could feel. He could feel Althea, who was there most of the time. He could feel the Dilaudid, the two doctors' gloom. And he could feel this strange, new, warm, and frightened weight of his brothers, both of them, just as he had felt the frozen thump and then the giant, slow-rolling weight of the deer, covering him, falling over him from out of nowhere.

SCORPION DAYS

WE BOUGHT the kif from a Moroccan kid—probably
a soldier—on the Tripoli-Rabat Express, handing over the
quartered dinar notes for the four or five flat-rolled *zagarettes*, clipped and trim and even. We stood facing him,
holding on to what we could, hand straps and seats and
backpacks, rocking, swaying as we raced through the date
oases at the desert's edges. We got it not so much for wanting it as for the bad way the kid had taken Roberts's joke,
Nous sommes Algériens, which made him frown and look
as if he were reaching in his djellaba for something harm-
ful. So we bought it out of shame, as a sort of apology. We
hadn't known how much the Algerians were hated, how

fierce the battle had become with them for the Spanish Sahara.

Roberts, whose instincts I later would stake my life on, had said the wrong thing, the thing that could get your throat cut. So we were forced into being supplicants, which in the third world meant that most essential sort of other humans: consumers, customers.

Roberts was red-faced, downcast, as the strong-chested boy stuffed the bills in the pocket of his gray striped robe. *Joie, jeu*, said my companion, searching for the word *joke*. *Le jeu est fait*, said the Moroccan soldier: The game is up.

The whistle blew. The stop was a garrison of the militia, and he got off.

The stops increased. More and more people got off the train, and the clusters of buildings thickened. I got out of my rucksack the books Halpern had given me, which I was supposed to bring back for the magazine and translate: Ahmed Yacoubi and Mohammed Mrabet, books whose loose, soft phrasing could build up your Maghrebi if you digested a line or two a day. Badi, my tutor, would ride the train with us from Fez to Tangier in order to correct my selections.

The books were full of invocations, benedictions, not just from North Africa but from the far West and South, from the Dinka and Pygmy tongues. I read some of them now silently to myself.

Somehow, when I wasn't watching, Roberts had put the kif in a loose, thick catalog of birth and funeral songs. I snapped it shut. We had come to Central, the great main station webbed in glass and iron.

Our hotel room looked out over the *mamounia*, the old tanneries and the drying and folding stalls that surrounded them. From there the lanes of the medina wandered up through the hills. The stink of the tanneries was legendary: a hellish, rancid stench that brought tears and jagged fits of coughing. And we had two windows of it, the price of a cross breeze on a humid summer night.

But it also masked any odor one brought to the room. So after dinner that night, Roberts opened the funerary and took out the sticks. As he lit one, I could see its oval circumference, and as he passed it to me, the brays of the donkeys pulling the tanning buckets grew louder.

The weed was ravishing. Beyond belief. My spine felt lined with something like a ridge of tongues, with honey poured along them, cooling and pulsing like the morphine wash they had given me once for kidney stones. The sounds of the prayer callers had started and mixed with the donkey brays and the creaking of the wood and ropes. It was the violet hour, the time the long day's haze made all the buildings' edges wash and seep up toward the giant, starless night.

There was a knock on the door. Before the sloweddown sound of it ended, the knocker had opened it, and

Roberts made a sudden gesture toward the window, pointing or violently pushing.

"Control," said the man who had entered. Behind him there was another man. The speaking man had large, scratched glasses and an open shirt. The one behind him had a narrow, sweating face, and his cotton *dhoura* was buttoned to the top.

The first man made a sniffing sound.

"Control?" Roberts asked, his left eyebrow cocked.

I watched the streams of sweat on the main man's neck. His hand was open in the air, a laminated picture on the right and crooked typing on the facing side. No badge. No gun. But we were convinced.

Roberts asked again. My heart pressed up against the sides of my ribs, like some sort of swelling fruit.

"Do you want to see . . . ?" the man's voice trailed off, and he made a clasping motion with one hand over the wrist of the other.

Roberts shook his head, and I saw now it was a sort of cooperation, a disarming honesty he was going for. Something incredulous and American. He bunched his mouth to say no disbelief, no disrespect intended.

When my eyes went out toward the roof, Main Man's did too. He waved his hand for the other officer to search it. But Main Man joined him when nothing presented itself, both of them leaning their palms on the sill. Then the lieutenant hobbled over and out onto the tiles, walking and crouching, bringing out a flashlight.

My heart was like a rabbit now. The seconds were long, dull flashes of panic. Looking at Roberts's hands, making sure they were open, I thought of my first near bust in the relative comfort of my own country. Mounted police had come down to a circle of us in Golden Gate Park, their horses stamping and chafing as one of the officers dismounted. We'd thrown the joint away, but their hands went through our shirt pockets until they found the film canister in Marty's. He was the one they took in. But we knew where to find him, and when, and how to go about it. There were no surprises inside the surprise.

The Control agents came back inside. They hadn't found anything. Main Man was sweating more, clearly agitated. Roberts looked over at me, and I could see in his eyes the fear of a plant, a drop, a thrown-down something they were about to dangle in front of us.

They both sat down on the desk chairs. They were ready to negotiate, for all I knew, on matters they had yet to propose—an offer waiting in a place they would haul us down to or had prepared in the room next to ours. I could imagine writing the rest of my travelers checks out to the two of them or going to their own money changer. Or worse: I saw myself locked away, outside the reach of diplomatic help, my twenties evaporating into something

I'd know later only as static time—a thing I'd never lived, a droplet I had never tasted.

But the two of them were winded from the search on the roof. They had nothing, and looking across the beds and desk and shelves gave them even more of a nonnegotiable empty hand. They struck us now, with their heavy breathing and heaving, sodden shirts, as cops too young to pull off a plant, rookies too green for crookedness.

When they had left, Roberts and I looked at one another, not speaking, reeling out of the fear we could sense in each other. After a minute or two, I could see his fingers shaking, a true tremor, like an old man with a disease. I had nearly shit myself, but what I thought was my own stench was once again the heavy offal of the tanneries, the air's own hideous thickness.

At first I thought Roberts was watching the spasms of his hands, which he certainly was. But I looked at the sight line he made along his index finger and down to the floor. He was pointing. The *zagarettes* were there in the middle of one of the squares, scattered like pick-up sticks, their paper color blending perfectly with the shade of the limestone.

Badi sat next to me on the harbor train, going through my notebooks, looking at the Maghrebi texts I had been working out into what I hoped was a lyrical English. The coral trees threw in a checkerwork of shadows through the windows. The dark patterns tumbled over Roberts's face, sleeping across from us in the breezeless compartment.

Badi said we had been the victim of a scorpion, *les scorpions*, hotel con men posing as federal police. We were going over some Dinka songs, and Badi made quick corrections as he spoke. He said we were lucky. Even young scorpions were rumored to be good at setups. We had definitely gotten two who were off their game, or, more likely, were themselves too high and disoriented to remember their routine.

Badi came to a song whose final lines I had not yet captured. He tapped his blue pencil on the already smudged, torn paper.

"Scorpions grow up in camps, in prisons themselves," he said. "They are like the Guardia Civil up in Spain or like Russian police. Good at getting criminals because they were hoods themselves."

The lines of the Dinka song had to do with cycles and recurrence. The "framing" couplets of the stanza spoke of rains that come, go away, wait in the place they have gone away to, and then come again. I'd gotten those two lines perfectly.

"They kill," said Badi. "Scorpions all lived in the camps of the French, not knowing from one day to the next if they would be around. So they are not afraid. They will make the move without hesitation."

Badi stopped his tapping.

"What happens to you?" I asked.

"I don't know," he said, "but there are places up in the Atlas. Riverbeds, full of bones."

He changed the words in the final lines to *man / Who is born, lives, and dies / Goes away to the place he waits in / And does not come back again.*

The cadence was gorgeous, the sounds of the Arabic spectral and cool, like echoes bouncing back across stone. I put my hand on Badi's shoulder, and he snapped the notebook shut. Soon he was asleep too.

It would be an hour or two before Tangier, and hours after that waiting for the Algeciras ferry. When I closed my own eyes, I saw the two men sitting in the room again. Then I saw lines and lines of the script I was learning, its sharp points and waving upward thrusts, like young grass just starting to come into its growth.

ROAD OUT OF

BABYLON

THE LTW, or light tank weapon, that seemed to rip out of the very air and lodge itself in Stephens's torso, was really nothing more than a small missile with rifling fins on its tail and a grenade charge in the tip capable of blowing up a large car or a truck.

It didn't explode, obviously, which was obviously our biggest problem. But that wasn't what we were thinking when the Somali jeep stopped long enough in the intersection for two teenage mujahideen to take aim at our patrol before we could even think to look up or duck into one of the pock-holed storefronts.

They were gone before we could return fire, and the two others that took it with Stephens were dead. Once we were on our feet, we dragged them into a roofless tinsmith's shop for tagging and called the medevac for Stephens, whose head I'd put on my pack bottom and whose eyes blinked at me nervously and then began to stare ahead, twitching spasmodically in the after-echo of the firelight.

He was only bleeding from the exit wound, where the brass-colored metal tip could be seen coming out from behind the clavicle. Other than that, the LTW was just a big diagonal lump lying under his gear and battle dress. He looked like a shoplifter who'd been trying to make it out of the store with a lamp stand or one of those cases containing an unassembled, segmented fishing pole. He looked scared.

There's nothing like the sound of an inbound Huey, and when the ambulance version with its big red cross came down in the dust of the same square where the bullets had come from, we ran with Stephens on a litter into the enormous, dark opening guarded on each side by a silent, black-faced door gunner. This suddenly was the happiest place you could imagine being, the solidest place you could imagine having ever existed, and everything about these sentries turning their weapons on their swivels seemed like the natural extension of some higher power's intervening fingers.

I'd stubbed my foot on one of the chopper's landing

slats. I didn't have boots on, and I bruise easily, so I kept my foot nestled in my lap when I found a place to sit down.

They secured the doors, and we were in the air very quickly, hitting a few rogue thermals, a crazy, rapid climb that made us wobble up and down. But this *was* the desert, I told myself, and the three-man crew didn't seem to be minding the bumps, or minding the fact they seemed to be missing their second navigator, a problem I ascertained from faxes of the cockpit chart that were scattered around and splotched with boot prints made from Stephens's blood and dust mixed up together.

I looked around. This was obviously a very large double-rotor ambuvac, not a Huey at all. Behind the cockpit was a sizable prep room—this is where the gunners had been—which could be used for a doctors' sink or for jumpers or rescue gear, and in the middle was a tiny marine-type head and the operating room, where I was for some reason sitting. The shafts of light that came in through the fuselage vents flew back in rapid bands of bending orange and had to travel a long way, as if through the entire distance of a long house trailer.

When we leveled out, the doctor came back to give me the bad news and then the really bad news. He was a young guy, couldn't have been more than twenty-five. There was acne across his forehead, which was almost all I could see of him with the cap and mask being one of those one-piece deals, a gigantic tubular ending of the upper body that made him look like a bright blue Q-tip.

He said—and why was he talking to me, was Stephens already prepped?—the field hospitals all along the Aden River had been burned and looted for their pharmaceuticals. This would have to be an onboard procedure. And he said that they had to get the LTW out of Stephens pronto because it might have a timing device, which could detonate at a certain altitude or after a certain number of hours. When I mentioned that we'd had incoming of these that had switch-off timers that worked the other way and went into battle lock after about thirty minutes, he looked impressed with this observation and nodded his head at me thoughtfully. But like most doctors, he was a step ahead of you, and he gave only enough pause to let you know you were being listened to.

"These are Pakistani antitanks. There's Arabic lettering on the tip of the round."

A shaft of light moved over his acne, making it look like some kind of red, wet wound.

"I've never seen one of these that shuts off. And we've got a lot to think about here. We're following the river, over our troop centers, and as I said, we've got to op on board. If it blows, it doesn't just kill everybody here. It blows a whole lot of this thing, maybe all of it, out of the sky."

I sat up straight until my ass was feeling the hum of the floor. "That's a whole lot of iron," I said. I didn't want him to think I hadn't been listening to *him*. "It'd be like that . . . what was it . . . Skylab," I said. And the thought of it all happening made me sick, made me feel like I was already going light-headed in the bathroom. "That'd be bad," I said, looking up at him, at his skin.

"Boy howdy, it'd be bad," he said. That phrase he used, the eyes giving their sort of smile, the soft accent—I had him completely pegged by this time. He was one of those cardiac cowboys from Baylor or Texas Tech, working off his school loans flying sorties into hell and patching up every kind of strange thing he'd never see again in a lifetime of civilian surgery. If he got us out of this, I thought, he'd deserve all kinds of high fees and golf items and exotic forms of consulting income.

A big groan came from Stephens. I could recognize the voice.

The doctor stepped into the head a minute, and I asked him if I should stay.

"Just stay out of the field," he said. The sterile field is what I guessed he was talking about. "Anything white or anything silver," he said. "And come fore and scrub up with us."

But it was too late for that. They were bringing in Stephens. Where did all these people come from; where had they all been sitting? They count-to-threed Stephens from his gurney to the table. Everybody was blue now, the lights blazing in the room.

Then they left again, leaving me alone in the OR with Stephens. They must have figured I was the closest thing he had now to family. I guess they wanted to give him a minute while the anesthesiologist got her materials prepared.

Stephens's face was happy, flushed pink, and washed clean. When the anesthesia hit this IV, I thought that would be it. But the guy started going on like my father, like some kind of insurance salesman on speed.

"How ya doin'?" he asked me.

"I'm fine," I said, grinning. "You're gonna be OK too, I'm pretty sure."

He looked over at the tubing, at the instruments, back at me.

"This thing, they gotta ditch it. It's, like, sort of still ticking."

"It could be or couldn't," I said. "We can't take the chance." I wanted him to get this outside the doctor's hearing, so the surgeon wouldn't think I was copying his spiel.

"Yeah," said Stephens, "those timers, you know."

"Yeah," I said, seeing a flash of water out the window. We were following the river, and the man wanted to talk.

"This thing is a Paki."

"So I hear."

"It's a Paki," he said again, letting out the phrase slowly. The lump in the gown was something awful to see. The swelling, the hematoma, had made a gigantic mound.

"It feels like a turd," he said, starting to giggle. The dope was starting to affect him, slowing down his voice.

This also made me laugh, and my fatigue made it worse. Soon both of us were cackling. Our eyes were getting wet.

"Like you gotta pitch a loaf," I said, just getting out the words.

And he sneezed (the drugs do this), which interrupted his laughing, and said, "Yeah, a big turd. Like they'll drop on Bombay."

And we lost it. We were shrieking. The anesthesiologist almost smiled. She tapped at his IV hose, getting down a good drip.

We were shaking from the laughter when he blindly reached for me. The anesthesiologist set down his arm, and I remembered about the scrubbing. I wanted to get to the sink, but he was talking again.

"That Satan," he said, "We'll get him." The anesthesiologist's eyes shot over to me.

She probably thought he was talking head, going crazy with the drug, which I had sampled by letting a droplet or two come out of the syringe tip. I knew Stephens was talking about the warlord we were fighting along the river. Comrade Satan, he called himself, and his people had names too. His specialty was killing IFOR troops and kidnapping UN personnel. He'd called his series of weeklong raids "Operation No Living Thing."

"Those guys always get theirs."

How could I not agree? I had my doubts about Satan, about our ability to stop him. His soldiers were thirteen-year-olds with fifty-caliber machine guns, high on the Dilaudid that was putting Stephens under.

But this wasn't my place now; I had to give him hope. He was no more thinking about Satan than he was thinking about the Mets. He was about to go to sleep with Satan's belly full of bomb, and bravado, of course, was the only kind of feeling I could pull out of what was left of my faith.

He was looking for encouragement, for a vote for his life. Not a vote, but a kind of passion, something he almost wanted to hear me shout. All the turd jokes, all the laughing—it was like he was here with his family. All our barking and our rolling was just monotonous family talking, assuring him he'd go on living in the world he'd always known.

The surgeon was in now, with two more assistants. A team of two men sat now catty-corner to me. They were in full battle dress with mesh vests and steel masks.

A box lay between them with its lid propped against it, no words on it, just a scraped-up, thick, olive steel vault.

The doctor had made the incision, and the assistants were setting retractors. One of the pilots stuck his head in.

"What've we got?"

Nobody looked up, but one of the attendings answered. "Subcutaneous lodged grenade."

The pilot's face turned white. I could see it go that pale even in the near-pitch black of the doorway he stood in.

"Is it active?" he asked.

Nobody looked up, and this time nobody said anything. He stood another thirty seconds, the rackety plastic door banging back and forth against his open hand. He looked in my direction.

"Well, fuck me," he said, and closed the door on himself.

Was I breathing in fumes of the dope from the air? Or just feeling the taste I'd taken from the line? I felt sleepy at the window, saw the river's far sparkle. Who, after all, ever really wants to die? The world seemed so good now—the sky bright and pulsing. Those mujahideen back in country, blowing themselves to vapor? This must be all they wanted: a calm place like this.

When I came to, there was a lot cooking, and by a lot I mean enough to give the Buddha some jitters. It was all too fast to follow. But I was family; I would abide.

Lifting my head up high enough, I could see that Stephens's chest was completely open, splayed from sternum down to crotch. I thought I was going to black out until I saw the tail fin wedged just under his pelvic bone. The surgeon was trying to loosen it while keeping its tip free of all the instruments and glistening tissue. One of the box men was giving instructions. To the surgeon! An ordnance grunt! He stood up to offer his pointers and then crouched back down and murmured to his friend.

I leaned forward. They were lifting. It was a sea of blood they worked in.

The assistants had their elbows on the white rows of sheets, gloves open, while Dr. Acne brought the dripping rocket up. He handed it to the first assistant, who then handed it to the second.

Then the box grunt reached out, signaling the assistant to keep the tip up, and when she gave it to him was when it slipped on them, started falling toward the floor.

Things slowed for me here, the Dilaudid kicking in. Or maybe my disbelief at it falling made my vision of it freeze. There was an arrow we learned about back in high school, the Greek philosopher's arrow—Zeno? Every piece of space it traveled was something separate and of itself. So how, the teacher asked us, if it was always at a particular point, could it ever get anywhere, could it really arrive?

It tumbled slowly in the light, and I hit the deck, and

my heart just stopped. I cupped my hands around my head and saw the box when I shut my eyes.

There were two clunks, maybe three.

It was battle locked. But I was trembling. And every one of us was holding prone. All of us, that is, except the doc. He might have crouched; I wasn't watching. But he sure was standing now, sewing Stephens up, staring straight down into him with his headlamp switched off.

"Shit," I heard him say slowly, when the long stream of red shot up. It was blood and coagulant.

"That thing clipped the aorta."

The two assistants were off the floor, and the box grunts dismantled the missile. They laid the round base down in the padding and pushed the lid tight, snapping the winches shut.

By now the three doctors worked quickly, the assistants bringing forward new tools. But it was a river streaming from Stephens, probably of spirit as well as blood. The three of them were looking worried and then panicked and then more tired. And they were soaked. They were dripping, their hoods black now with sweat.

All this was the really long part, but my tensions kept me awake. The doctors sewed him up under a single, slow-ticking lamp. The stars were out in the porthole, and under the lamplight the thick, lumpy beta packs glowed dark purple.

Stephens died before we got to Addis Ababa. I stood honor guard, straight-backed and bawling, beside the gurney they had returned him to. We landed at dawn, the sun pinkening his sheet. There were minarets in the foothills of the mountains around the airfield, and the signs along the tarmac were lettered in Aramaic. This too was a fierce and different world. And I felt tired and drained enough to be dead.

Losing some people can make you lose all of just those kind of people in the world: lovers, say, or a kind of friend or relative. But losing other people at a certain time can make you lose the whole world, lose everything, so that afterward you can go on living but as little more than a walking dead thing, a bug in a shell, occupying all of your attention and time with the simplest of tasks and the truly fruitless job of rethinking how it might have gone differently, how the bridle might have pulled another way.

And places are like that too. Somalia had become such a place for us first-time combatants. I can still see it perfectly out the thrown-back panels of the black-pocked chopper door, the closeness of our deaths and the whiteness of the heaven we were being thrown toward like a bunch of mindless, new-made mayflies.

ANGEL OF SLEEP

WAITING FOR the junior college bus, I see a van of
drug enforcement men, the DEA, come for the couple, the
really young couple, who live in the place above Trader
Joe's. You can tell the DEA by their windbreakers, a lighter
blue than the navy-colored jackets ATF agents or sheriffs
wear. Drug men usually have their suit shirts and ties on
underneath: natty, dark, and groomed up like the Efrem
Zimbalist Jr. of old. They are like that, the DEA. They look
like they have just had to leave their desks or a business
appointment for the bothersome, headachy dirty work of
actually bird-dogging something in the field. They look
like they only have enough time to be making the bust
they're out on, just that window, and everything has to

keep spot perfect so they can get back to their quartered squares of newspaper and still-warm cups of coffee.

One man, the lieutenant, stands toward the rear like a cop up on a berm in a traffic stop. His jacket bulges out in back from the hard angles of an automatic pistol, one with a large magazine in case they find themselves all of a sudden in the suck. A couple of sergeants bang on the door. A third sergeant has the warrant in a yellow-tinted plastic VeloBinder the color of pee. The breeze whips the folder cover into a flutter, that metal racketing sound like the sides of a storage shed in a strong wind. The man puts his hand on it to make it stop. The lieutenant feels around behind him and touches the bulge, runs his fingers over the column of the barrel under the *zip* sound of the rayon. Then he adjusts the pistol he has on his belt, which has a badge on the top flap of its holster. They all wear reflector sunglasses, oversized, like the celebutants on VH1. One of them blond, they have clean, full, ungreased hair, not the brush cuts you expect from *CSI* shows.

There are so many like the Trader Joe's couple that I have a hard time remembering them now. They are Romanians, not much more than children, from orphanages that were abandoned after the fall of the president in 1989. They grew up in the streets of the capital; one street I remember from a documentary was called Little Money Street—*little* as in *no*. Packs of them ran together, running scams where they distracted visitors with news-papers until one of the smaller ones could come around and lift out a wallet, yank away a purse. They were dark skinned, and the cameraman thought them Black Sea people, *people of color*. Everyone tagged them for gypsies at first, "Roma." But the darkness was just dirt. It was the grime of a life lived with your face turned up at the sun all the time, sleepless and never washing, splattered with the muck of food thrown out the back of ministry kitchens and eaten quickly.

These packs of kids tore up rags and dipped them in toluene, a solvent that gave its boost from chemicals mixed with the kids' own perspiration and saliva. Toli rags, they called them, and the grainy film was filled with groups of kids sharing them, ripping them up and break-ing them down even more, into little squares like the wipes that come in tinfoil at takeouts. They stood or walked or crouched in front of the camera, holding the rags over their noses. Some of them put these smaller pieces over their noses, sucking them against their nostrils, like in a contest to see who could hold their breath underwater the longest. After a few minutes they would wobble in front of the lens, fall over, fall down in groups.

I am assuming this Trader Joe's couple were once toli kids, but it's a safe assumption. The only other way they would have gotten a habit would have been as

Romanian government people's children, with access to heroin and synthetic opiates that became a medium of exchange in the twilight time between the Big Man's fall and whatever government they have there now. Maybe they were just that. It made getting out easier. You could get your visa and drift from club to club through the capitals of Europe until you were out, really out. A true street kid had to smuggle *himself*, ride in plane wheel casings or ship containers, somebody else, alive or dead, beside him.

I do know that the man, the husband, had gotten disabled on a punch press, making Saturday night specials in one of the little mall factories in Lake Elsinore. His Kaiser doctor got him OxyContin, a limited scrip, only for a short time, and that was all it really took. Bucharest came and laid itself down in our spotty little high desert, the Dracula scrim settling in like mist around the tin cans and tumbleweed. They were buying Green Monsters—twenty-milligram Oxy capsules—from kids here in the valley for $80 a pop. Mr. and Mrs. Romania started to just live for the stuff. It took the place of light and food and oxygen. It was larger than their life and anything in it. It was larger than love.

They had a three-year-old kid, a girl. Sometimes they took her to the park, and you could see them with her on one of those spinning platforms that look like giant lazy

Susans. After their habit started, they didn't come out of their house. They didn't open windows or go out to the market. Dust built up on their cars, and their TV antennae fell over, its flat black wire gone slack.

Then the kid died. It ate one of the capsules that had fallen on the carpet. Even in an adult, Oxy can stop the heart for long, terrible seconds. It has that kind of power. The lungs switch off. The respiratory system crashes, falls down in a blast of neuronal wind. The father and mother were trying to revive her when the paramedics got there. She had fallen over as soon as she picked it out of the carpet. Her skin had turned a rapid, cold, mottled blue.

≈

The two sergeants without the warrant talk between themselves and try to decide something. Then one of them goes back to the van and carries back a megaphone, white with a red tapering mouthpiece, up to the living room picture window. He stops, looks down, swings the thing between his hands. He looks for a minute like he might lift it up and break the window with it. Then he takes it back to the van, and when he walks back toward his partner, his holster is open, the badge on it flip-flopping brightly in the sunshine and his fingers wrapped around the pistol's stock. He lifts the other arm to his face and speaks into his wrist.

I hear the bus coming up over our hill, and as the men close up around the door, they have their guns in their right hands. The lieutenant doesn't bother with the machine pistol and has his sidearm out, the stock of it resting on his shoulder. The warrant is folded in the newspaper hook under their mailbox, black with a little gold eagle on it, its wings spread, like something you would see on a building or on the back of money. The four of them are frozen there, like plastic lawn sculptures, like those little walking families of deer.

When the bus stops, brakes hissing, the horrible white elderly dialysis transport doors opening, I climb up and walk back my usual four rows. *Four corners, four winds.* I don't take my eyes off the men as they start to yell out their orders. But it's all muffled under the bus sounds. I can't hear anything they are saying.

No one comes to the door. And though she knows better, the bus driver stays stopped, her door open, pretending she is waiting for somebody else to run up and get inside.

After the long minutes, with the men looking like they are about to just kick in and sweep the place, and with all of us ready to duck, the front door pulls back and the shadows of the living room swallow up the white space the sun has left there. At first I can't see anything in the tall opening. Then the small head starts to materialize behind the screen. It's not the mother or father, but somebody else, somebody younger, a tall twelve-year-old or somebody in their early teens. Maybe a cousin or neighbor who came to help after the funeral. She or he, I can't really tell with the spiked hair, stands talking to them for a minute or two. He steps back from the door as it opens. The last man in picks up the warrant, still rolled in the mail rack, and puts it in his back pocket.

As the bus starts rolling, I pull out my *Songs of Innocence and Experience* and see the Gilded One standing in his column of fire, couplets racing along under him as if they were clouds he were standing on. The parents went on as normally as they could after their daughter died. Neither of them went back to work, but they wouldn't have been able to anyway with the way their habits were. They had been tagged by an undercover man, maybe caught on a surveillance tape, for something involving the baby's clothes. It was her pants and shoes and a snowsuit they were trying to sell, for more pills.

UNDERTOW

GILLIAN WAS relieved when his friends Matt and Sally invited him to dinner the following night. They would have Maddie come, a Swedish girl they had just met at a Mabou Mines production in Soho. Matt joked to Gill that there had been enough lag time after his break up with Michelle, and though Gill faked a laugh, he indeed found himself reassured, calmed and grateful for the presence of friends who could be counted on to fill an anxious emptiness with an unexpected invitation.

He lay the receiver down with reverence, remembering Auden's lines about the kindness of others, the safety one found *in the harbor of their hands.*

He was really out of the backwash with Michelle, and it was the story he was working on that bothered him now. He was happy with his opening tones and settings, but hadn't been able to get his characters up and moving around, creating the nervous footsteps of plot, the narrative trajectory. He remembered Nabokov's edict that his creations were his slaves, supplicant for their existence and trembling at his every direction. But Gill wanted to give them freedom too, unexpected divagations that would surprise both him and readers, whetting their stalkerlike curiosities.

But his characters had done neither. They had neither obeyed nor disobeyed his orders. They'd stayed frozen, inert, their backgrounds and habits and other general life stuff fleshed out, but all of them refusing to undertake motion, refusing to oblige him with kinesis.

The character as couch potato. The character just sitting there, breathing, looking back at him for guidance. Which he avoided, staying fixed on the phone. It seemed at least to have a life, a form of active existence, sending dust motes up behind its blinking, buttoned console.

～

Matt opened the door, the soft stained-glass of the ceiling lamp throwing a patch of blue green on the Berber carpet. One of Matt's eyebrows went up.

"Man, the devil's beatin' you down."

"Don't start," Gill said. "The wounds are many."

"And many," said Matt, "are the crimes."

Pulling his jacket from his shoulders, Gill saw someone, he assumed Sally, running back through the hall in a black leotard and T-shirt, giggling. But there was another set of footsteps, a murmur of bare feet where the hardwood started.

"Boy wounds? Girl wounds?" Matt asked.

"Boys and girls together. I'm having a form of block. Character immobility."

"Screen all frozen up. Shit. I'm sorry. Let me get you a drink. You need fuel. You need . . . You need . . ."

"To get them romping," said Gill, laying the jacket in Matt's hands. Matt opened the closet door, and Gill, again appreciative of the old code of manners he always found there, thanked him, helping him wedge the weighted hanger into the bank of blazers and cloudy quilted vests.

"You need," Matt said, "to *meet* somebody."

He called Sally's name, and she came out, brimming, freckled with her New England freshness, already holding Gill's drink.

"Laphroaig," said Gill. "You remembered."

She handed it to him as he kissed her, and, from behind her back, she brought out another tumbler for Matt.

Sally had just motioned him into the kitchen when

Maddie appeared. She was most definitely Swedish, with blazing blond locks in a straight chop like Gill had seen on Asian girls at the Genius Bar. Her face was ovoid, perfectly, beautifully symmetrical, and her blue eyes sparkled as she reached for Gillian's seeking, frozen hand.

In the instant she looked down, he let his eyes go to her body: long-armed and thin-legged in her shift, her breasts pushing out as if molded by a dirndl.

"We're making Mojitos," she said. "We're Mojitos girls, me and Sal."

They walked in and sat down at the table, where dumplings and vegan *faux*-meat items lay steaming.

Maddie said she'd already heard a lot about Gill, that she'd heard he was an intellectual. When he asked her who told her that, she said nothing, then mumbled something about present company, shrugging her shoulders.

She picked up her Mojito and downed a half, three-quarters of it, like a thirsty frat boy.

Gill watched her move eagerly into her food, plopping half a blini into her mouth as Matt and Sally twisted noodles with their forks, throwing out statements that Maddie grabbed and ripped at as fiercely as she ate. When Gill complimented the mayor's criticisms of PC recycling, she snorted and dipped her head, rolling her eyes. The banter between them grew: strident, ferocious, with their hosts trading looks of approval as the guests continued to dominate, like chosen waltzers a crowd of dancers had parted for.

Gill liked her; he liked the idea of her. He loved her mannerisms, the appetite, the fact that she looked so much different than Gill's usual choices, which Sally could describe generously as waiflike and, when weary of his pickiness, with one of the names of a German concentration camp.

After dinner they sat smoking, all but Sally, who kept at the Mojitos. Matt had brought cigars from a federal judge he was in front of a lot on cases now and who had access to customs seizures. But Maddie was a European in her smoking, cigarette after cigarette, sucking the hits in and holding them for long, self-conscious seconds that let the watcher know this was a drug for her, a means of transport like any other.

The more they talked, the more Maddie softened, asking what it was Gill wrote, nodding with interest at his answers, with what he took to be earnest sympathy. She dropped her cigarette on an elaborate rug beneath her chair, the coal flying out, bounding like a grasshopper. When she tried to pick it up, she squealed as it seared her fingertip. Gill, in a single, smooth movement, steered the sparking ash over into her empty drink glass and looked at her finger.

"Ice," he said. "Put a towel on your lap and keep pinching pieces of it between these fingers while it melts."

Gill told her he was setting some story scenes in some of the old parks of Chelsea and the LES. He'd be walking through a lot of them the next day. Maddie watched the ice turn into droplets, squeezing, rolling the cubes as she continued smoking with her unburned hand. When the new cigarette ash dropped she caught it in her freshened glass, and when Gill nodded in mock admiration, she asked if she could come with him, that she had a day free from her ad sales job.

She gave him her cell number, and they arranged to meet in the morning at City Bakery. The neighborhood always gave Gill the shivers, dead center as it was in the agent and publishing gulch of the Flatiron District. "I know the place," he said. "Yeah, good choice." When she stood up and put the cap on her pen she smiled, her wet eyes full of the rum's vapors, the blues around her pupils swirling and darting like fish.

⤝⤞

When they met in the morning, her eyes were red, as if she'd been rubbing them, and she smelled slightly of some kind of wood smoke. But he liked the way her hair was mussed, its punk spikes confirming the hardness of her charm, cutting away the remainder of what Sally called her Heidi vibe, her mountain yokelness. He pointed to the fruit bar on the second floor. She did an approving pirouette, grabbing a wet tray from the stack and drying it on her jeans as she climbed the stairs.

She missed one step, wobbled. She grabbed the banister.

When she lit into her muffins and fruit and downed her coffee the way she had her rum, he saw the red vessels in her eyes. She caught him, turning her head to the side to accommodate his stare.

"You're high," he said. The smoke smell was hash, the sweetest, most perfumed kind.

"Drugs are good," she said. "That's the motto of a friend of mine's website. His agent's website, actually."

Her plate was almost empty.

"The *tagline*," she corrected herself.

Gill marveled at her. He imagined the two of them in a souk together in Sidi Bou Said, one where he'd been too often alone.

"Weed really isn't my cup of tea." He waited a second and added "so to speak." She was too young to get the joke.

"Don't you find," he asked, "that it makes you . . ."—he didn't want to say *insecure*—"more self-scrutinizing?"

She nodded eagerly, holding her cup up and pointing downstairs to the lines of warming beakers.

He watched her from above as she filled both cups,

her movements of studied recklessness and pure, curious bravery. He had no idea how close to the edge she would travel, but he saw her as the perfect true-life hero, balanced, just barely, on a crest of dread.

He tapped the bottle of pills in his jacket pocket as she sat back down.

"Of *course* I get freaked out. I think all kinds of things, like my diesel mechanic uncle in Cleveland is going to come and kill me. But I maneuver it. It's worth the buzz."

He drank. She'd put in a cinnamon blend.

"And just fighting it, hitting against those feelings is a buzz. Like kickboxing."

"Have you ever tried opioids? You know, painkillers?"

Her neck went down in complicity. "I'm *dying* to," she said.

He pulled the bottle out. Shaking it, he figured, would be too scripted.

"Well, well," she said. "This *is* a surprise."

"You working today?" he asked.

"From home," she said slyly, pointing down to her bag. "That's home." She brought out her phone and tilted it. "That's home."

She couldn't take her eyes off the pills, and he knew the lift in her voice was coming from the sight of them, the way they lay like little clouds inside the dust of the orange cylinder.

"Well," he said, "I'm just walking, working on the story. You could still make your calls. The phone just won't work in the subway."

She picked the bottle up, looking to where the label had been scraped away with something unsharp, primitive, like a key. "I'm not even going to ask where you got these. Don't tell me some dying grandma."

He extolled the convenience of it, explaining that unlike what she'd spent her early morning hours doing, there was no need to look for a place to take one.

"We could do it now," he said. "They pack a wallop. You should start by just splitting one with me."

He felt suddenly older than her, with the small guilt of proposition going down through his shoulders like the branching, sharp after-weight of exercise. He imagined what their table must look like to others: a slightly older editor, a geezer roué going after the new editorial assistant.

But she was already taking one out and splitting it, snapping the creases of its score lines. She brought it to her mouth and noticed her cup was empty. She nodded toward his coffee, half full, and as she lifted it, she handed the other half of the pill to him, closing his fingers over it and squeezing his palm.

They had been walking around Tompkins Square Park for a while once it kicked it. The dry fountain they sat in was tiny, and it was as if they were back at the upstairs bakery table.

"It's like a tide," she said, "the way it moves almost completely away before you've felt it."

Gill was used to the feeling, the loopy tug that teased your energy away at first, then stretched it out and relaxed it, turning it into something restful and elevated. Soon it was tingling through his frame like a lining of the inner body, an underflesh that hummed and crackled like a sheet of static.

She pulled out a cigarette and he lit it. As the flame went out, he rejoiced in his good fortune: getting her out on a single request, hers really, and his enlistment of her as a Boswellian accompanist. Actual bones and blood were more predictable than characters. He'd done good by these instincts, by his guilelessness with a true human. And good came from good: Maybe his creations would follow suit.

He saw that she was letting the Marlboro burn down completely like the night before, the ash falling on her shoes.

Then he saw it: a cloudiness in her eyes, a creeping puzzlement.

"What *is* this stuff?"

"Dilaudid. Synthetic opioid."

"What is . . ."

"Did you ever see *Drugstore Cowboy*? The scene when William Burroughs plays the defrocked priest and pulls out a vial of it, liquid, and says, 'Ah, yesssssss . . .'?"

The ash was close to burning her fingers. She let it drop. Then she stood up rigidly, like a soldier called to attention.

"It's giving me dry mouth. I need something to drink."

They walked toward an Egyptian restaurant with figures—jackals and cobras—painted over its door. Walking hadn't seemed to help Maddie. When she sat down, she gagged, picking up a phosphate that had been left there by the couple walking away. She gulped it down. Gill looked at her, but she wouldn't meet his eyes.

"What *is* this stuff?"

"It's a strong postsurgical anesthetic. An analgesic. A painkiller."

She didn't look up when the Nubian waitress, delicate featured and swift, arrived at their table. Gill ordered two iced mint teas.

"Why'd you give me this?"

"You wanted to try it. You wanted to take it with me."

She lit another cigarette and let it burn, not putting it in her mouth.

"It's given for postoperative pain," he said, wondering

if language with a technical cast could calm her the way it would calm him, coming from a doctor.

"But why?"

"Why what?"

"Did you *give* it to me?"

He stretched his hand to hers, and she worked her bracelets back to let him hold her wrists.

"Maddie. You wanted to try it. You were *excited* about trying it. It might feel a little funky for a while. But you've got to maintain. Just give it time."

He knew what she was feeling: the surges of panic and nausea, the calm periods, the resuming, galloping pandemonium. It was more cerebral than most PKs. It wasn't just body dope.

"What's it going to do to me?"

"Nothing, nothing but give you a buzz, the buzz you liked a while ago and will like again. It will come again. Just let it work."

She said nothing, laying the cigarette out flat on a leathery, cloud-bordered menu.

"You've gotta trust me," he said. "It won't do anything to you physically. It's a prescription drug. It's real medicine, not something that came out of the ground."

The waitress came back with the teas and looked at Maddie and saw things were wrong. She looked at Gill as if he were a kidnapper and she, the waitress, had discovered something enormous and illicit.

She put the teas down, and Maddie untangled herself from Gill's grip. She put her small hands, prayerlike, around the frosted tumbler. Gill saw the pill's powder under the thumbnail she'd used to pull it apart.

"Are you really a writer?" she asked. "Are you really doing this research?"

"Yes. Everything I'm telling you, everything I told you yesterday, is true."

"What's *happening*?" she asked, her eyes filling with tears.

"Nothing is happening. We're on Dilaudid. You're acting like someone from out of a—"

"What," she said. "What? I'm acting like someone from out of a what am I acting?"

He meant to say something like a soap opera, but her eyes were filling with a violence that was making him forget things. The awkwardness in her speech was something he had read about in the *PDR* and neurologist's descriptions. Mirror statement, it was called, the first phrase of a question repeated in its predicate, always hostilely delivered, like two sides of a jagged-toothed trap waiting for the listener's weight, the listener's question, to trigger the springs.

"Are you writing a story, really writing a story?" she asked, picking up his notebook.

"Yes, of course I am. I'm certainly trying."

"You're going to put me in it. The story. It's why. We're. Here."

She was rifling the pages. Then she picked it up and ran her thumb through their uneven edges. The notebook's sad emptiness made her more suspicious.

Paranoia, he'd read, was also a side effect, the kind of obsessive self-regard people got on hash and weed. Her eyes blazed back and forth between the scribbled and empty pages and his face.

"You'll write some shit about me here. You'll make up someone that sounds like me, and then people will know."

The word *know* rang in his ears like a high bell. It made him think she'd spotted something in him. She'd noticed something that was only sometimes there and only part of a larger set of traits, but which the paranoia had fleshed out, puffed up, given a poisonous, iridescent color to.

He put his hands back on her wrists, and though her eyes still sparked and blackened, she didn't pull back, didn't flinch. He held them tightly, then loosely, like a doctor checking a pulse.

"You've got to trust me," he said. "I won't hurt you. I won't let anyone hurt you. They'll be patches where you'll really feel good again, and in five or six hours it'll all be over."

"I've got to walk around," she said. "I've got to get some air."

He knew this was a bad idea, and knew he had to convince her it was. Anyone she ran into would see something was wrong. People were nosy, especially of women walking away from men in a huff in restaurants. He was afraid, if really asked, that she would exaggerate: He'd slipped something in her drink, a date rape drug, a . . .

But it was already too late. She put down a five and stood up again, soldierlike, and walked toward the door.

Gill ran after her. She wasn't at the bar or anywhere in the back of the restaurant. The black corridor leading to the restrooms and supply larders was empty, the corners of its ceiling blowing with cobwebs.

When he got to the end of it, he saw her standing by the pay phone next to the back door, but the second she entered his sight she pushed the handle and went out. She'd been trying to use the pay phone—its short, silver cable was still swinging.

She stood out on the street, searching through her bag, unaware he was watching her. When he came outside and she saw him, she was pulling her cell phone out of her bag.

"I need to make a call. I need to talk to someone."

"Maddie, Maddie, talk to *me*," he said, following her down Second Avenue. She wasn't evading him, but she wasn't slowing down. She turned down East Twelfth Street, and he picked up his pace. She took longer, more careful steps, as if to let him know she wasn't running from him.

As he closed in on her, he could see she was pecking crazily at the keyboard, first with her finger and then both thumbs. The shock of her hair swayed with agitation. He knew what it was: She'd forgotten all her numbers. If she was switching to an address book, she'd forgotten how to run the function. He felt a blip on his own phone: He knew addresses were logged by entry time, and that his number, which he'd given to her the night before, had to be one of the most recent ones on her phone.

He pulled out his phone and lifted it, showing her the lighted screen. "Tell me a number, I'll dial it."

This too went against his better judgment. Anybody receiving her call and who knew her would be able to tell something was wrong. A 9-1-1 operator would be able to tell. They would be able to trace her, find her wherever she was standing. Find him.

She shook her head and looked back at her device. He was relieved, but only for a second. She'd hailed a cab. He could try to wave the driver on, but that would puzzle and probably panic the cabbie. And if he tried to pull her out, now that she'd opened the door, it would be worse.

The guy would be on his own phone in a second, calling the cops.

When she got in, she said nothing to the driver. He could see the cabbie leaning back, gesturing with his hands: "Where to? Do you have an address?" Gill was level with her at the back door. He looked in to where something had been resolved: The driver put the meter down just as Gill called her name for the last time. Her head was forward, her face, her forehead bent toward the cab partition.

Then she was gone. Where the car had been was now only stoops and railings, garbage bags, the remnants of what rats and passersby had discarded.

He breathed deeply, deep, deep breaths of relief. It was the relief of a man who had stepped back from an abyss, feeling gratitude for his own immediate life and flesh, unable to think of the companion who had vanished, seconds ago, an arm's length in front of his face.

In his own cab, he leaned his head against the seat and started the slow, particulate task of talking himself out of any responsibility, or at least of most of it.

Getting out and walking up his steps, he went down through the catalog, ticking the items off: She, after all, had been the one to invite herself along; *she* had presented herself as the drug aficionado, the dissembler of straightness, the pilgrim of altered states. He remembered how she had grabbed up the bottle and dumped the pill out herself, cutting the score line in half like a junkie-adept.

The manuscript of the story lay by his monitor, and he went over to it after he'd taken his clothes off and put on his sweats. He tapped away at a paragraph. He took up a sentence and looked at it, turned it around in the light like a hard rock crystal. He gave a character, heretofore immobile, the slightest of pushes. After a minute or two, he revived another, gave them the gentlest direction, and the two encountered. He found the pair talking, talking incessantly, their conversation emerging in brilliant, whiplike sparks after weeks and weeks of blockage, like the sun's edges flaring out from behind the moon that had eclipsed them.

After twenty minutes or so, revived by this success, encouraged with progress, he found himself drawing a blank on a couple of minor characters. And then he recalled something. By now he was much more used to the drug he'd taken than any newcomer to it; he'd adapted, built up a tolerance, learned to navigate its surges and rests. But still it left gaps in his brain bank, an inability to call up the simplest of details: a character's features, his initiatory, identifying mannerisms. Lying down on his futon, the picture became clearer to him: This was a drug that could wipe out whole swaths of existence from the mind, entire categories of memory just as you took in its full effects, just as the tide—as Maddie would say—was overtaking you.

He was drifting off, remembering these long-past, engulfing blanknesses, when he realized a novice like Maddie could forget everything—where they were going, how they could help themselves, even where they lived.

The monitor went dark. He turned his head aside on the pillow. Then the phone began to ring.

PRISONS OF THE
KING

CAMPO SIETE is one of those all night cantinas on
the trucking roads that run through the Isthmus of Tehu-
antepec. These are the blue highways on the map, tiny and
mangled, made of the same hand-laid stone the Mayas
and Toltecs used for their ghostly altars and pyramids.
Coming out of the northern cities, they rise through the
scrub-thick, brambled lowlands into the mountain foothills, dipping and twisting until the road breaks down
into gravel in the high, cold groves of pinnacle spruce and
new-grown juniper. You are only on the peaks a few hours
before you begin to loop back their shadowed, southern
sides, level by level down again into the warming, haze-
draped altitudes. Finally, after hours of stone road again,

you come to the great ports the roads were built to feed: Veracruz and Coatzacoalcos, the Caribbean Babylons, their invisible columns of deadly sun and beehives of people tearing away at the jungle's green.

But it wasn't day when we got in. It was a midsummer night, that still, pitch tar spread out with the flashing gravel of the southern constellations. The door to the Campo stood under a single *santas* lamp, the paint rubbed away and the wood worn down by the many hands of impatient drivers. You could hear them inside as you walked up, a muffled explosion of light and noise as the latch gave way.

It had a long bar, like the famous one in Ensenada, but wider, so everyone sitting on the high stools who wanted to and was out of sight of the bartender could bend over when it got to be too much and stretch their stomach and chest along the bottle-dotted wood. The drivers were in front and the locals in back, never the twain meeting, we knew, the drivers seeing the townies as provincials, lazy and backward—Indians stuck here by unshakable lethargy and fecklessness.

But the drivers were only kidding with each other now, the fat one in suspenders in front razzing the others about the weigh stations in the South, how they'd been wasting their time there without bribe money, fools to be stopping and putting up with the oldest and most obvious and transparent of bureaucracies. I could get most of this if I listened carefully, but I needed Mac, whose Spanish was better, to get the rest.

One of the drivers—they called him Suspenders—was going down the line of *campesinos* with his electric box. The grips hung dangling from their wires. Some of the farmers jumped back at the sight of them, as if the box were a vicious dog or a reptile.

The drivers were going for it now, most of them drunk enough to take a few jolts, their backs flattened against the bar and their wide thighs tensed around the stools by the current. We'd seen some of these guys two nights before at the warehouse in Campo Seis, dancing with obviously underage girls in pastel tu-tus and baby-doll pajamas. These outfits had something like bustles, masses of netted fabric that swayed like ghostly, glowing bells. Men like Suspenders danced with them sleepily, clutching the girls' shoulders with hands that looked like the giant, bent forefeet of mantises. Some of the girls had hard, sloping eyes and looked retarded, their hair sprayed into flat, sharp cones and triangles.

The boxes were standard macho regalia for the drivers and for all Mexican men in bars like these. Maybe for all Mexican men, period. It was 1973, the days of the first

Chiapas rebellions, what Warren Hinckle was calling the New Time of the Lawless Roads. For all we knew, Echeverría and the cabinet passed them around at state dinners, easing back in their chairs to use them as mettle testers of other Latin dignitaries. I thought for a minute that it may have even been the way the defense minister was "accidentally" electrocuted by his brother in the palace bathtub a few weeks earlier.

These gizmos were simply large, smudged gunmetal boxes, flat hued and thick with prints, lined with rivets, and inside you could see the colored balls of wire and flickering, cobwebbed cathode tubes that lit them. A crude dial was pasted to the top, probably a speedometer or gas gauge from an old tractor, the needle black and the arch of hashes black and numberless.

The box looked heavy but really wasn't, because Suspenders, the guy holding it, would move from stool to stool and customer after customer drunk enough to take it while another man held out the true and actual lightning, the little copper claws at the ends of the wires that looked like jumper cable grips. Box carriers I'd seen in other bars had always, like Suspenders, been short and fat and plastered at the top end with enormous balls of greased and matted hair. And the grip holder, like now, was always taller and dapper and gaunt: the face man, the presenter.

What he presented was electricity, that rarest of tropical juices—the hottest and fastest atoms, the surest maker of men. All maleness here seemed ready to be so measured, and though the very idea of such a thing struck me as boorish and repulsive, I decided to ride with it, to watch it through the clear, clean lens of the anthro-tourist.

After two or three stools, the duo got somebody to take the grips, to fork out the pesos at some *campesino*'s egging and lay his drink down long enough to hold the pair of copper jaws. The subject up for inspection now sat very rigid. He held the grips straight out at an angle and gave some kind of unseen signal to Suspenders, who wiped his mouth with the back of his hand and bent over and started twisting the knobs.

The man lurched at first, then hunched and steadied himself, then lurched again and sputtered and shook until the wetted curls of his hair wagged around, growing so runny with sweat that they stuck to his head. There was a lull where the subject breathed quickly—in, out—and the wetness on his stomach and chest spread the length of his shirt. Then the presenter turned the voltage up. But the customer wonderfully, wonderfully *held*, his hair smoothing out and his eyes clinching tighter, maintaining, soaking up the heat of the charge . . .

The second customer was taller and much more polished, dressed like a *pachuco*, a dandified townie with a moustache and hat. When he was handed the grips, he looked at them skeptically, shaking them and turning them upside down. The men beside him were respectfully silent and ran their hands on the stubble of their chins. When Suspenders tried to return the setting to zero, the *pachuco* waved him off and said, "*este, este*": He would start at the level the first man had reached.

This man simply rattled. His hair rose like snakes. "I'm reminded," said Mac, "of Frankenstein's monster." But after a few minutes, this man too adapted. He evened, he leveled. A calm came upon him. He was churning cold fire into warm macho fuel.

And on down the line they went, from drinker to drinker. The *campesinos* especially sucked up the voltage like bulbs. I expected them to come away amped up and jittery. But they left the game mollified, like sleepy, fat dogs.

~

Large, green-dressed men wearing bulky black jackets and belts full of metal and plastic hardware filtered past one of my eyes, blurred more with mescal as the hours wore on. Every two or three people through the doors would be one of them, this squareness of their coats and the long bills of their caps giving them away. Chiapas was far away, and the rebel leader Comrade Marcos hadn't yet come to power. His radiant face had yet to rise from its sea of machetes and maize tents. But the guerillas he would arm had started to gather, here and farther northeast, on the gun running and dynamite highways. Echeveria's vicious army had come early to ferret them out.

With my other eye I could see Mac, watching the box bearers with mockery and envy. How often in those days I misread a face, an attitude, and attributed to people qualities of mind they didn't possess. But I was pretty sure I was right about this new crudeness in him, this strange embrace of some old manly code of values. He'd changed in the two years he'd spent in Carolina since we left our Cleveland high school, I going off to Berkeley and he apprenticing with a scab, cold-weather carpenter crew, a roughshod but meticulous group of fast-working stoners. And he'd changed even more in these four months we had traveled, smoking and snorting, growing inward and cold.

For my money, it was purely the weed he was smoking. It was that and that alone that made him clam up and snap at you when you asked him questions. It was almost impossible to get him, glassy-eyed and paranoid, to ever look at me when we talked. All I ever saw was his riveted profile, the stringy, wet hair falling over scratched glasses. He had the trail-worn look of rock stars back then: Neil Young, the Allman Brothers—full sideburns, flannel shirts. We all looked like that. But he looked it in spades.

I'd had to watch this profile all the way across the country and then down into Mexico for two solid months. He'd been jittery, hunched up over the wheel, staring at the road and lip-synching the Deep Purple songs that came on the radio.

"I could do *this* shit," he said now, stabbing his finger at a glass. He pulled up some pesos. They were new ones, paper singles etched with Aztec pyramids. They shook in his hands, which were bunched into fists that he pounded on his knees.

I must have made a face or something, because he stepped off the stool, pushed my arm aside and turned around to glare at me. "I'm going to *try* this fucker," he said, loud, so I could hear him over the music. He slapped the leg of his jeans, which he would drum to songs. He was trying to focus his eyes on me, but all I could see was the scratched glass filmed and whitened with steam.

He whipped his pants again and coughed. A puff of weed smoke came out.

~

More and more soldiers were coming in now, not obviously through the door, but just appearing in the crowd. After a group of them went by, I saw Mac now at the box.

How quickly Suspenders had gotten to him! He fastened hard on the grips. His straight hair had fallen forward and one of his boot heels dug into the rail.

I waited for the first jerk, but I could see that the Mexican had the dial on already. From where I sat the needle looked high, straight up through the numbers at whatever that was, five or six. The last *campesino* hadn't gone any higher than four.

Mac was unfazed. If he was feeling it, he wasn't showing. He looked just as calm as when he'd been doodling on the napkin. Sure, he watched the box, and with something like intent. But it was more the cold stare, the pure, vacant doper's trance. The hooch, the pure, battered wastedness—something had drained him. It was fire passing over already-burned ground. The problem was he couldn't drop them. He just stood there holding on. Suspenders just peeled them off his hands, and when the grips fell on the counter, we could see the stripes on Mac's palms.

It was then that his shaking started, the faintest tremble when he walked. It was in his upper arms, under the loose denim of his shirt. He came back and settled beside me. He bent his head and closed his eyes. His whole body was moving by then, and somebody must have mentioned the burns. He put his hands, palms down, very softly on the table, in a dark, bright, and slow-spreading puddle of beer.

I wanted to stay awake with him, but the mescal was

strong. It was shutting me down quickly, covering the room with fog. Through it Mac sat with his hands on the table, his teeth chattering as more and more soldiers came in. I blacked out when Suspenders walked toward me with the box.

Mac was gone when I woke up. More of the black-jacketed soldiers were milling around. The *campesino* regulars were thinned out and getting thinner, walking out to their trucks, coffeed-up and starting on the footpaths toward home. The fans were off. The candle lamps were blown out.

I had to piss, bad, and got up and headed for the black tunnel of hallway that wound out to the loading zone and parking lots. The mica sparkled on the tunnel walls and stayed with me in the afterimage as I leaned, eyes closed, in what was essentially a closet, sinkless and mirrorless and roofless, but very tall and quiet and lit only by the moon.

The mescal was still very much with me, because I made a right turn and ended up in the lot, with soldiers suddenly getting up off the packs and boards they were sitting on. They could see I was stumbling, and this is why I imagined some of them were scattering or turning their backs, climbing up into the cabs of trucks parked over pools of what looked like oil.

The truck that faced me was filled with stumps or limbs, something wooden and ripped-looking dangling out the end of its covered bed. I had a hard time focusing on it and for a minute was seeing double. Then I took a few steps back and looked again. One man sat on the side rails behind the cab, watching that end of the tarp nervously and taking care to keep it smoothed out. But he couldn't stretch it over everything. Somebody was telling him not to, or, more likely, it was stuck.

There was laughter and then groaning and spitting from the other trucks. Someone was coughing into the can they drank from.

The more I focused on it, the more one of the wood chunks in the truck looked softer than timber, more pale, somehow, in the light of the kerosene lamp. They had bands of scarring—like I'd seen on Mac—on their bottom sides, and at the end of each were short, spread nubbins or thin, tendril-like clusters, delicately opening. The whole stack of them became pale and clear now as I stared at them, hands open or toes spread, muscles as hard as rows of string in the sparkling dew. All with the stripes, all with the brand, like meat you lift up from the bars of a grill.

Around the back of one of the other trucks I saw them: the metal boxes, stacks and rows of them gleaming in the lamplight. One of them was connected with a bigger wire to some kind of generator. They were exactly the same machines the drunk men had used in the contests. But with the arms and legs I saw in the truck now, some lit by the moon and some half covered by tarps, they had been used differently.

I started nodding finally, swaying. The last of the meal I had eaten in midafternoon was coming up quickly, and I ran toward the bathroom. But there were too many soldiers in the doorway, blocking it to keep the inside safe for whatever they were doing. The long, thick stream came up out of me, burning, spraying across the mounds of gravel.

The only thing I know about the direction I ran in then was that it was away from the trucker's shacks, because they weren't there—only open road running by scrub acres and burning patches of banana groves, with little tar-shingled bus shelters built up next to the curb every several hundred feet. The fumes of the booze were still getting to me, so I laid down under one of them. I spread my arms and moved my head until a glob of pebbles wedged up into a mound under my neck.

I thought of the strangeness of seeing the maggoty side of a people jump up out of nowhere after long weeks and months of their seeming goodness. It took the wind out of you. My mind ranged back through the cities I had come to love, the ones whose very names had lulled me: Guanajuato, San Miguel de Allende, Taxco with its silver basilicas. But even on their streets, in the alleys between the decrepit shops, there had been the dusty-windowed coffin stores: scores and scores of baby caskets in frilly white, a world so ready for death's suddenness, for its heavy paw.

I turned my head aside and retched again, but there was nothing in me.

I spread my arms wider, making the motions we used to make as kids making snow angels. The gravel felt good under me: cold, immaculate, and dustless. A wind started blowing, and the tiniest pebbles, as tiny, it seemed, as dust or sand itself, started blowing around me, up through my pants, around my bare head, out over my dampening hands, which I bent down and looked at and opened and closed again as if working a miracle.

It was as cold as snow itself, a heavenly powder. It made a quiet like the quiet of newly fallen drifts on the flanks of mountain roads as you entered their cities again, the deep stillness of their swirled and whitened hillsides.

But before I drifted off, my heart jumped up again, exploding softly, puddling and bubbling its warmth. I was afraid to fall asleep for fear of dreaming again of what I'd seen. And I wanted to know somehow, by some sort of sign, that Mac was all right. I wanted to hear the tread of the old high school boots I had come to expect in the halls of C Building. As much as I hated him now, zoned and stammering and badgering me about some new nothing every day, I had to be sure that whatever I was learning about this place had not made him part of it, and that he would be the one coming back, looking for me.

PEACEABLE
KINGDOM

WARNER WAS not surprised when the men started picking up the conches from the wet sand and throwing them against the boulder walls. He winced and stepped back when they laughed at the shells exploding, and then had to turn away when they drunkenly guffawed and groaned at the soft, pink, oblong globs of living tissue meandering slowly down the crevices of rock.

But surprised? No. Warner wasn't surprised. How could he be? It was entirely in keeping with the character these stewards of business had presented to him now for the two long weeks they had traveled together through the cities and islands of Thailand.

Warner had been stringing for *Forbes* for some time now. His knowledge of economics had moved from passable to mildly competent, and they sent him to the semiconductor CEO conference in Kuala Lumpur with ample perks for a non-staff writer: a room at the Peninsula (where his subjects were put up), a driver, a translator, a generous expense account. The conference itself was at the Jockey Club in the new Petronas Towers, a structure that had long fascinated him with its ghostly, double-towered silhouette.

Haw. Haw.

The laughter Warner heard was devoid of energy, of any trace of the zest that had animated their business presentations.

Hawwww. Shit.

The man who said this steadied himself after his throw. An enormous explosion echoed across the length of the beach, back toward the cabana above the high tide line. Warner looked again at the boulder wall, at the shards of bone-brown cockle rattling down.

The laughing man was William Parker, who had boasted of four girls at a time in his motel room on Pat Phong. Parker's older, thinner friend Childs, who had steered these later days of the trip into pure sexual tourism, came over and laughed softly at his bent-over, breathless companion.

"They were bigger in the Cooks," he said. "The fuckin' things sounded like a twelve-gauge."

Other men were seeing how high they could arc the shells as they threw them. Some spun themselves around like discus throwers. Some tossed them underhanded.

"Warner, get over here," said Milford. Milford's company had gone public and blossomed across the NASDAQ on a handful of rumors, but then had stayed the course, immune to the bubble burst at the millennium's end. Milford he thought of as an intellect, a reading man, though he was not sure why. When Jack stepped back from Milford's entreaty, the older man didn't press the matter.

Ka-THUMP went the shells now, louder against the cliff face as the sound of the surf subsided. "Aw, Jesus," somebody bawled. Another round of laughter rolled over the waves.

It was Hunter, the biggest man, an Alaskan. He was the keynote speaker, a computerizer of fisheries, and one of the leaders of some of the more salacious side journeys. He had gotten too close on one of his windups and had fallen facedown in the sand. The creature's pink matter lay splattered over the top of him like vomit.

Steven Fell came over and stood beside Warner as Hunter picked himself up. Fell, who Warner also took to be a kindred soul (was it the spectacles?), mumbled insults at Hunter under his drunken tittering.

"Like watching the white elephant take a shit," he said.

Hunter turned around to face the men. Some of the sand was dry and came off quickly as he brushed it. The muddier stuff began to smear, with each new streak provoking laughter.

"I'll say," said Warner.

"This is disgusting," said Fell, though Warner had clearly seen him throwing. Two of Hunter's men, very highly placed in his company, came forward to help clean their boss with their handkerchiefs and sweatshirts taken from around their waists. Warner knew them only as Bob and Bub. He knew they would do anything, including divest themselves of their last garment, to clean up the man.

"Warner, what's up with you?" asked Purdy, a particularly drunken software designer. The deeper question was bothering Warner—not why he wasn't throwing, but why he wasn't trying to stop them.

It was not just the futility of such a request. Warner had simply convinced himself that it was not his place. He was the writer, the observer. He could no more step in and stop the slaughter, he told himself, than if it were humans they were killing.

Maybe he could do it in the sarcastic shorthand that passed for speech in their delirium of rum and liquored fruits and cakes. A humorless strategy would surely be rejected, would get him slapped down and ostracized, perhaps even make it back as a "perceived negative" to his editor. "Thou shalt not piss off thy copy," the Pacific Rim slot man had told him. "Business reporting rule number one."

Warner saw now that Hunter had recamped. He and his men picked up more of the shells and, in a face-saving gesture of revenge, began throwing them faster at the walls, standing farther away but tossing them up like pop fly baseballs. Their frequency now over the utter silence of the lee water sounded like peppered gunfire or firecrackers, sounds folding in and out of themselves with overlapping cracks and echoes.

Some of the men were wobbling. Some fell down. "I knew you were a southpaw," Bub said to someone whose shell didn't make it.

By now the rock face was a wall of gore. The creatures themselves had a muscular texture, with veins and long strings of marbleization running along their twisted bodies. They had black, dotlike eyes or sensors that slid down in disarray. Warner remembered his childhood dog's penis arousing, stiffening and glistening out of its sheath. He thought of the way potato heads, decked out by him and his sisters with buttonlike ears and eyes, would cave in upon themselves after a few days in the dank air of the potting shed.

As the men got up and brushed off their hands, Warner noticed the stains on their palms. Some of them walked over to the long, troughlike sink of the cabana. Its left side had eight or ten pipes with double spigots. Far to the right, under the canopy, honey-colored bottles of beer stuck out of a pile of ice.

Some of the men wandered over to the sink and simply stabled themselves, staring into the running water. A few looked up at the waiters, some of whom would carry them all in motorboats over to the restaurant later. The hired men averted their eyes and shuffled, smoothing their towels and aprons.

But most of the businessmen leaned down and scrubbed their hands vigorously, trying to get off the sand and the underlying stain. The stain stayed, though the water lightened it. It dried into an umber color, darker brown than it had first appeared. Its shade was like the sienna hue on the hands of Berber women Warner had seen in Morocco, the symbol of the future, the Fatima.

Scrub as they might, no one could get the whole of it out. Most of the men simply lathered their hands and fore-arms or splashed some of the bright water on their faces. But some of them, perhaps the very drunkest, cupped the water in their hands and slowly drank it.

Once everyone sat down to tea and the sherbet was brought out, most of the laughing stopped. Mounds of shell fragments lay up against the bottom of the cliff.

When the tea and sherbet were finished, the men grew very quiet. But the amber and transparent liquors continued to come out in fragile snifters, and every one of them was downed. Some men drank from others' glasses. Some pulled the childhood trick of pointing the glass's owner to something nonexistent and then drinking his shot before he could react.

Warner looked over to the only other movement in the cabana besides the waiters' comings and goings. Hunter was sitting on a bench behind the trough. The straps of his pocketed travel shorts hung down between his legs. He had a shell in his hand. With the other hand he was pulling ferociously at the pink thing inside, twisting and angling it out, grimacing, cursing.

No one was laughing. Nobody was even looking at Hunter. They were all turning their heads to where the cabana man was pointing to the motorboats.

All Warner remembered about the water taxis were the sleeping men, heads sprawled on the life preservers they had refused to wear. The water of the headlands was a blazing, almost iridescent azure. Waveless and vast, it covered the occasional coral bed like a limpid blanket. Warner tried to stay awake by looking over the side. Before he nodded off, he saw the Gloriosa Yacht Club shimmering in heat waves over the plain of blue. The docks were calm. The needle-boats were covered with their numbered canvases.

Where did these men get their energy? Surely the same combination of stamina and obliviousness that got them where they were accounted for their revival now in the shuttered dining room of the Gloriosa. Warner was feeling the effect of the three beers he'd drank on the other side and ordered now an equal number of espressos. The men were vibrant, jousting. They asked for Champagne and were brought buckets of it.

Rumor had it that Saudi princes were in an adjoining wing with their usual entourage of prostitutes. Parker and Childs had a plan to crash their party, but Hunter said it would have to be finessed, as the Royal House's bodyguards were notoriously trigger-happy. Warner had read in his own magazine of the sexual appetites of the House of Saud. It eclipsed their hunger for deal making and preservation, or seemed so much a part of it that flesh was there to bribe and bless even the smallest of their transactions. The men, Warner knew, were jealous. Jealous of the Arab men's wealth and of their satyr's luck. The CEOs certainly didn't get where they were by letting anyone out-fuck them.

Some of the men were holding Champagne bottles by their bottoms, draining them just as the appetizers arrived. Oysters and lobsters were presented, and white wine in clay pitchers dotted the club's round Chiang Mai logo.

Childs stood up, holding a glass.

"I propose a toast to the Arab boys yonder," he said. "If they can fart and send my barrel price up $50, they've got to share a little of what it got them." Laughter. Parker stayed seated but lifted his glass and seconded Childs.

"If they keep those girls under so much cover, they've got to be something special."

"Who can we count on for some firepower here?" asked Hunter. Four empty bottles of Champagne stood on his table, presided over by Bub and Bob. Hunter had called the wine "pig's piss" and sent it back, but one of the clay pitchers was empty and laying on its side. Green puddles of wine pooled on the tablecloth.

Warner's table could have been worse. As the noise grew around the room, he appreciated the softer timbre of this group's voices. Milford sat next to him, still ordering anisettes and sambuca. Danson was to his left, as much an enigma to Warner as he guessed he himself was to the others. All Warner knew was that Danson had made millions, lost it all, made it back again. He spoke only of his home, his horses, the wife and daughters who attended them. To Danson's right was Lichtenstein and Weber, Lich's aide-de-camp and fellow pub crawler. Warner guessed them to be the only Jews in the bunch, something he felt the others were sensing.

Lich and Weber were big figures in San Francisco's arts scene, patrons on a scale of the Rockefellers and

Heinzes. Their latest play was for vineyard land in the North Bay, which made their tolerance of the mediocre wine surprising.

They were also rumored to share women. Warner didn't believe it for a minute. He simply could not picture the fastidious two following one another into the breach. Each of them was immaculate, clean-shaven. The whites under their nails were like pale, clear quarter moons. They wiped them after each squeeze of a lemon, after each oyster.

Purdy started singing some club song, waiting to see who else would pick it up. Warner had read of this practice in accounts of the Bohemian Grove and Olympic Circle retreats. It was a way of spotting insiders from a place that was still exclusive but getting outsized, unnetworkable. Four or five others joined in the melody, like monks taking up a chant. The music had an Alpine flavor. It was beautiful but fell strangely on Warner's ears—a wintry, piney melody echoing out over the tropical water.

Milford fell back in his chair as straight as a statue, landing with a thud that sent the others into an uproar. He seemed to have a smile on his face, and his eyes were certainly open, but there was a stiffness in the way he clung to his glass, as if he were making some effort at self-mimicry. Purdy walked over to him and sprinkled water on his face, which led to more laughter, and then went back and sat down.

Milford lay there breathing heavily, his face wet. The smile was still there, and it looked like an almost enviable way to rest.

Bob relished his role as jester to his boss. He stood up until everyone could see him and then sat back down. Gripping his empty glass, he pushed his foot against the table leg until gravity brought him backward, crashing just as Milford had.

After a round of applause, others began to join in. Each tried to appear stiffer and more nonchalant as he fell. Some did not take time to empty their glasses. No one got up once they were down, and Warner saw everyone's chest heaving like Milford's had, apparently unable to contain their laughter. A third of the men in the room were on their backs in chairs. They looked to Warner like the plastic Siegel sculptures he had seen at the Berkeley Art Museum.

Purdy was the next to go, bringing the jesting fallers to nearly half the room. Everyone at Warner's table had done the same, but Warner trained his eyes upward and away. The waiters kept their distance. Men in the back were wheeling entrees out in little towered carts. It was going to be a long dinner for them.

It was then that the three high streams of blood shot up at the same time from Purdy's face.

Two gushed out of his eyes and one from his mouth.

The blood splashed down onto his cheeks. His chest was motionless, his limbs relaxed.

As the other men went down, Warner noticed other sounds amid the laughter and clapping. Many on the ground were gagging now. Some grabbed their collars and their movements stiffened. Then blood started shooting from more of their faces, like water sent up from lawn sprinklers.

Warner's legs were frozen. He wanted to get up, but whatever his mind was telling his legs was not working. He watched the blood on Purdy's face begin to pool and thicken.

The waiters were running out toward the men. Some of them spoke languages different from others, and one had to gesture to his assistant to make a telephone call.

Still Warner did not get up. Every one of his subjects was now on the floor. Most of their faces had suffered the red explosion, but a few had not.

Warner found himself thinking back to the rock wall and the pile of conch tissue that had built up in mounds. Some of the creatures had not burst apart when the shells broke and had rolled in single globules onto a level place.

Warner wondered what would become of them. Would they be able to get back into the water and build new shells? Could they crawl into others that had been abandoned? Much of it, he figured, would depend on whether the rock wall stayed in the shade or eventually got sun. If its rays hit them, even for a few hours, that would be it. They would wash out in the tide, dry and brittle, floating away on the foam.

Something like a flashbulb popped in front of Warner's face. A waiter was slapping his hands just inches from his nose to get his attention. Then the man cupped his hands around his mouth and yelled.

Warner got up. He *did* know CPR, or could remember it. But the bodies around him were still. Their heads were like mantles of trampled poppies, and the blood was beginning to smell.

Some of the men jerked and trembled both before and after the blood came out. Many of them had simply choked on it in the final phases of the hemorrhage. But the bodies of those who had lain the longest were stiffening too quickly for rigor mortis. Warner had heard of poisons that did this, but never of ones that caused blood to spray.

Warner looked around the room. The only table that showed signs of life was Hunter's. He and Bub and Bob's faces had begun to bleed. But they had a lighter, lesser film of it. And their chests were still moving.

Warner pulled Hunter away from his chair and stretched him out. He wiped the large man's face off with his sleeve, and bent down to close his nostrils and cup his lips over the open mouth.

Warner stopped. He saw the stain on both of Hunter's upturned palms.

The waiters were screaming hysterically, roaring, running in all directions. Warner looked up at the table and saw a napkin lying perfectly folded under a salad fork. He grabbed it and threw it over Hunter's face. He closed his eyes and knelt down until he could feel the outlines of the lips, and then he started to blow.

SELF-PORTRAIT WITH WOUNDED EYE

THE FIST came straight at me from just under the man's chin, not out from the side or up from underneath like an anchor punch, but straight on so as to be unnoticeable from the back, like I'd heard muggers held their guns in the neighborhood—the pistol butt tight against their own sternums so it would look to distant patrol cars as though they were standing, just talking to their victims. There was no need for him to do this, of course, because we weren't out in the open but in the long hallway's entrance to the kitchen of the Yorkville apartment I was living in with Teague. It turns out it was simply the style in which this guy threw a punch, like some clear ray of primordial energy coming straight out of the voice box.

Teague had run out of the apartment after leaning out the window and throwing water four stories down the fire escape onto the marine and his barbecuing family, drinking beer in their T-shirts and listening to Elvis sing "Blue Christmas" too loud for Teague's taste. It was 1979, and Teague, just back from England, was a CBGB's regular, and brooked no historical continuity between his music and the King's. The man and his friend or brother had climbed the escape, smashed in the Second Avenue picture window in our living room, and come to stand in front of me. Me, innocently drawing bathwater after my cab shift. Their drunken haze and the barbecue smoke made me indistinguishable from Teague, who by then was a block or two away.

I said, "My friend did it," and pointed down the hall. The man said, "Yeah, well, give him this," and the little wall of four solid fingers cupping the hidden thumb shot toward my left eye before I could even think of turning my head or ducking. Then another came so quickly that my blood splashed against his fist, and his friend came around to the side and held me from behind while Marine kept punching, slapping, kicking my sides and stomach and hips. His friend had me up against the window, and for a minute I thought they were going to throw me out.

But they didn't. They kept me right there in the kitchen,

six floors up, until they were finished with me. They ran out when they figured the slugs and the sounds of me hitting the pans and the table were going to be heard by other tenants or maybe even someone across the courtyard. I smelled their wake of beer breath and sweat and could see their blond hair wagging almost merrily, like the hair of schoolchildren racing away from a prank they were trying to disown. I slid down the wall until my thighs slapped into the pool that the tiny streams and then much larger jets of blood were sending from my face.

Cogency is a welcome visitor when you are injured. You think and act much more clearly than you would expect. Though I kept pressing dish towels soaked in cold water against my nose, and though I tried not to stand too much or get up too fast, I didn't call anybody or treat myself in any way so much as I *cleaned*, cleaned the walls and dishes and countertops that were dripping with my blood. I kept the tap on and soaked and resoaked the towel in my left hand and pressed it to my face, but with the towel in my right I crept along and squeegeed the drops and growing ponds of my draining *sangre*, my very life. It was if wiping the walls free of it would wipe the wound closed or begin the healing faster. Amidst all that chaos, my mind had the blessed rage for order Stevens sang of, and order seemed cleanliness more than anything, an erasing of causes by lessening results.

Running the water calmed me too, the constancy of its hiss. But under the burn that its cold gave to my face was the greater, bulging tingle of the real burn I couldn't ignore, the numbing and clotting of the hematoma that was swelling up under my cheeks like a grapefruit. That too was probably another reason I didn't step over and look in the bathroom mirror. Even that early I could sense my frightfulness, that I might faint in confronting my own reflection. What I didn't have to see gave me a sense of shelter. A look at what was really there would blast things open, let in a flood of panic.

In the middle of all the wiping and spurting of blood I finally—What could it have been? Three minutes, five?—called my girlfriend, Ronni. She lived a few blocks away on York, and it was there that I spent most nights. She had been urging me to live with her, to get away from the irresponsible Teague and settle down into one house, etc., so I expected this admonition again right off the bat on the phone. But it didn't come. She did, in a cab she had dispatched for Lenox Hill Hospital, whose driver fidgeted at the prospect of blood stains, of hauling a brawler away to his well-deserved stitching.

I shouldn't say there was *no* admonition. Ronni held me, like Jackie cradling the splattered president, and I watched her long, ringletted hair and big Odessan pupils with the one good eye I was able to lift from the pinkening dish towels. She stared straight forward and shook her head slowly, giving directions through the blur of darkening streets and newsstand lights, and in the few times she looked down at me she had to blink nervously, wincing and turning away with a jerk.

They kept her out of the OR triage they used to operate while the interns clipped X-rays to white screens, prepping me with Codacaine and Betadine, wearing pained expressions themselves at how much I was swelling. I imagined myself as a rubbery mass of creases, empurpled and horrible, rising in silence under the faint light like a blood-stenched mushroom.

I liked my surgeon, a young guy named Lefkowitz. You need direction in times like this; you need to be ordered. I wanted to sit up, and he told me to lie down. I wanted to talk to the observing med students (I was deemed "good trauma"), and he told me not to talk. His response to all my prognostic questions was that I had "a lot cooking."

"You've got a massive subdermal hematoma with complex septum fractures, bones and cartilage punctures through the nasal shaft. You're gonna go into shock if you don't stay warm."

"Am I going to be all right?"

"You've got a lot cooking. You've got a lot cooking."

The interns stood staring, leaned forward, leaned back. This was clearly a man they had come to see *work*.

He snapped on his gloves. He cooked. I blacked out.

I only woke up once. It was when Lefkowitz was suturing the *inside* of my nose, the vascular membranes the bone and cartilage had ruptured. I don't remember any pain at the needle going in, or even the slightest sense of contact. What made me uneasy—almost nauseous, or more nauseous than the anesthesia was already making me—was simply the sight of the long black thread being pulled so far out of my nostril and then hooked back in. The oddity of it: that any tissue could be stitched on the inside. But when I thought about it, I realized it must happen all the time.

I saw faint traces of my reflection in the TV screen while watching the evening news with Ronni. She stared straight ahead the way she had in the car, her eyes frozen, the point being, *this proves it, come live with me and be my love, and bad things like this won't happen to you ever again*. The big bands of gauze didn't look so bad in the mixed opacity of television images. Only when shots of night or the vastness of gray Iranian bridges and turrets came on could I see within them the obvious mummification of my face. Then, or when Dan Rather wore a *dark* cardigan (he was doing that then, along with President Carter), suddenly I could see the giant bandage that I was at the bottom of the screen, superimposed on his solemn, trustworthy Texas profile. Rather was in his very, very weird late-seventies phase at this time, staring intently into the camera at the end of each broadcast and saying, "Courage." I took this to heart and decided the time had come to witness myself full-on, in the full-length mirror of Ronni's roommate's closet door.

The first time was horrible: I looked like something out of a World War I hospital daguerreotype. The bandages weren't wound around each other like in the old movies, but lay in patches about four inches square, pressed over the bridge of the nose and over my left eye. The flesh around them was going from purple to black and was so swollen now, so bulged with subdermal blood, that I could think of nothing but the boxer dogs I had grown up with, their wrinkled, glistening reek.

Once, when Ronni was out of the house and the pain was mild enough to keep my hands from shaking, I lifted the bandages to see what was underneath. The nose was twice as wide as it should have been, stuffed with wooden splints as thick as clothespins and themselves wrapped in layers of gauze. The blood on the cotton was constantly fresh, as bright as the petals of a rose.

But my upper cheeks and eye sockets and maxillary sinuses were a minefield, that hideous and frazzled fighter's mask of blood crust and slime. The gouges and cuts showed Marine must have been wearing a ring. There was a star-shaped laceration on my nose bridge that was filled with wildly branching, tiny, hair-stiff plastic sutures. Another cut formed a *V* so perfect it couldn't have been drawn better. No stitches here, just a butterfly bandage. The rest of my skin was like the terrain of planets you see from satellite photos: dark and murky, an uneven ground of great black holes my pores had swollen into.

I put the bandages back. I took a walk along the river, wanting to catch the midsummer, early evening breezes in Carl Schurz Park. It would be the first of many I'd take to pass the time, to heal, to not have to look at myself. Walking, a summer of it, and of riding the trains.

I would like to be able to say I took fortitude from this time and used these privations to accomplish new things and set new directions for myself. But in truth, the assault sent me into a downward spiral and a new sense of insecurity about where I was headed. I had some good pieces of writing going, but I was starting to question whether I had the talent that would enable me to outrun time enough to make its development worthwhile. I was basically like everybody else at my age in New York: twentysomething, fresh out of college, bartending and cab driving, trying in the few unexhausted hours left to me to turn away from the easy outs of law or business school and begin to build the arc of something significant, if not giant. Preparing to risk everything, or to talk myself into risking everything, in a single throw.

But these wounds were becoming the end rather than the beginning of hope. Illness and injury, supposedly catalysts to the artist, can also seem like the fists of the heavy world beating down on him. Pain like the pain I felt, pain and its physical *distortion* of myself, seemed like society's reminding bludgeons of what it did to its poets, even more to its would-be poets.

I rode and walked as I healed, and wrote and wrote and wrote, but my spirits sank under the heat and the gloom of the summer's rain, the gritty thunder of the subway tunnels and the fog of half-sleep the Darvocets spread into me. I grieved for my inability to put a sentence down, turn it around, make it right and be able to feel the joy of making it right—my sureness of touch was starting to drift away, dissipating in the alternating currents of agony and then chemical bliss that lapped and sloshed inside me as I moved. I began to fear a psychic emptiness or monstrosity growing to match, to be *caused* by, my physical one. I feared becoming the gravest of Nietzsche's aphorisms, the one I always skipped on the pages of *The Gay Science*: "What someone is begins to be revealed when his talent abates, when he stops showing us what he can do."

What someone is. The store windows shot my image back at me. That's what I was: a crumpled and patched-together and spiritless thing. In pain like this, the body is not so much the cage of the spirit as the spirit itself: the flesh presses its batteries into the heart, the whole being is pounded with the same hot blade.

These days I thought of suicide, the first time ever in my life. It was the last year of the decade and Elizabeth Bishop had just died up at Harvard. Her lover Lota Soares, the Brazilian architect, had swallowed a bottle of Valium upon learning of Bishop's affair with one of her female teaching assistants. Bishop wrote the glorious "One Art" then and only lasted another year and a half herself before dying, some say, of a broken heart.

But it was her poem "The Man-Moth" that obsessed me during my convalescence. *The Complete Poems* had just come out in the peach-colored FSG paperback, with her watercolor drawing of Merida on the cover. I carried it everywhere in my jacket pocket, dog-eared to the poem's two pages of mysterious stanzas.

It struck me as an explanation of suicide by an artist, the tremendous temptation to end the agony of his other-worldliness. It was a chronicle of the frustrations of leaving the earth, written just for those for whom nothing earthly would do. I was drawn to the poem's title soon after I bought the collection because a moth was one of the ani-mals I could imagine myself as then: the filmy, lighter-colored dressings surrounding my darkened eyes, the almost furlike softness of the bandages.

The lines that haunted me, to which I felt too close to even read, were the ones that speak of self-destruction and nonexistence as diseases the Man-Moth had "inherited the susceptibility to." Those and the lines about the death object itself: the electrified third rail of the subway, which ran along one's normal, well-meaning tracks of iron like a "draught of poison."

The book itself became my draught of poison, the Iseultian chalice I had to lay down like a hot coal from my hands on the bus or subway seat beside me. The whole sec-ond page of the poem made me delirious with fear. The final stanza seemed unnecessary; I judged it could have ended with his staring, hypnotized, at the unending silver trail that drew him and repulsed him at once, the very definition of dread.

The way up is the way down, they say, and Bishop's poem was as somber as it got for me in the week before the dressings came off. Art is life affirming and transfiguring sure enough, but sometimes only by putting you up against the door of death, borrowing from death's authority a part of the power it needs to work for what it says. Years earlier I'd had a Spenser professor who told us to avoid certain passages in *The Faerie Queene*, where the devil entreats the knight with the luxuriance of hell. We should only avoid these stanzas, the teacher said, if we felt we *already* "might want to hurt ourselves." That is, if the impulse were a disease to which we were predisposed.

Things shimmered and pulsed for me in this last week before the unbinding, walking around the city in anticipation of my new face. While pain meds were supposed to slow perception and movement, I found them to at least sharpen—to the point of exaggeration, maybe even monstrousness—things that I gazed out at from the breath heat and darkness behind my eye slits. Objects came at me with astonishing vividness and clarity, radiating, shining with a lamplike back-light.

And watching my own reflections forever altered my sense of my own appearance. I was barely past twenty then, just leaving the self-conscious agonies of adolescence: acne;

wild hair; a sallow, pasty torso and a gangly lower body. And while many people, especially girls, come out on the other side of all of this with a new robustness—healthily self-imaged, if not resplendent—it awakened in me an appreciation of the freak, the physical outlier. It led me to seek ways of looking at myself and others as *unnatural*. Before, I had been a tidy, engaging Golem. But now I had the inverse flair of the deformed, the newly minted monster.

If anything, I awakened to the mutability but odd *finality* of appearances. Just like the crumbling, constantly reconstituted city around me, my face was changing daily: My eyes got clearer and receded, little frostlike filaments of dried blood dropped away, falling down into my lap like dandruff. The flimsiness of 1970s Yorkville mirrored my face's changes. It was a proliferation of mixing images, all startling but all intangible. Sometimes, in the rare night I would spend back at the scene of the crime, I would look out in the morning to see the building next to me reduced to rubble, a pile of rocks or sticks tied up with ropes, left out for the sanitation men.

Lefkowitz smiled at the sound of the snipping scissors, the shells of stiffened cotton falling down on the examination table between us. Nothing was permanently damaged but the *inside* of my nose, the snakelike river of septum I have never seen, not even with a speculum, and thus have never had corrected.

I married Ronni, and I'm a lawyer now. A writer-lawyer. The stuff I wrote back then I kept but can hardly look at. The stories were like lengths of rope I had to climb to get where I am, but which had to be tossed away, kicked with sure force by the last foot to leave them.

It was my displacement from myself that haunts me when I think back to what I was after the beating, the removal of myself from myself that jumped back at me in reflections. I was that power-sapped Nietzschean, but at the same time I wasn't—I couldn't accept myself as such a thing and stood straddling the two images of robustness and deterioration. Whatever we wish for—art, riches, love—we wish to be well enough to wish or not, to continue wishing. We wish to be made whole.

This must be the reason that on the A train once, about the third day out of the hospital, I felt queasy when a similarly damaged man came and sat opposite me. We stared at each other in disbelief as the doors flew shut and the next station was announced. When the light in the car dimmed, we unlocked our stares and turned away from one another. I noticed that he shook his head exactly as I shook mine, that he was dressed basically the same from his bandages down, and that he carried in his undamaged fingers the same small, peach-colored book.

TOLAND'S CHAIR

ENIS KNEW how much the English liked the new land he had bought. For years the boy had worked for the man at the other, first farm, whose old house they were "cannibalizing"—his employer's words, he wasn't sure what it meant—and taking to the higher, brighter new farmhouse on the new parcel. The English had always used Enis and his other Amish neighbors for building projects, but Enis felt he knew the English better, could talk to him easier, and sensed that there was some reason or other the man himself always came first to Enis rather than to his younger brother, Noah, or for that matter to the elders—Enis's father and brothers, all still capable of heavy construction work.

Enis knew the English liked the newer parcel for the house and for the barn—the first farm had none. But it was the location—the exact location on God's compass—that had caused the English to buy just the farm he had bought, just the piece with the long back *T* ridge that sloped downward to the fence line of the adjoining pasture. That land contained a racetrack, one of the greatest and most famous in the country now, built forty years before on a whim by an auto dealer in the village and laying smack in the middle of the North-Central Ohio farm country.

Though Enis had never worked for the English during a racing weekend, he knew the land was increasing in value as the track drew in racers from all over the NASCAR circuit and tens of thousands of people to watch them, like people in movements he'd read of in pages of scripture. Enis's uncle told him that the cars their people had foresworn were changed by special builders into machines of almost unbelievable power, made to race on the wide gray ribbon that stitched the hills he could see when the English picked him up at their farm and drove him along the willow-bordered frontage road to the English's new parcel. The uncle nodded his head the way he did when he talked of wars and television and other English inventions— disapproving, condemning—but with the same look he had when his aunt brought a dish of new pheasant or grouse to the table, that identical eager glitter of hunger.

Some of the farmers, all of course English, had let the companies put up signs for oil and tires, helmets and asbestos driving suits. And after that came wider billboards for beer and tobacco, with pictures of half-dressed women standing next to giant replicas of products, rubbing their hands along the sides of the magnified objects. All of the signs said the name of the track—Mid-Ohio—somewhere around the product and its demonstrating, human doll. All of them were brightly colored, tinny, and prone to rusting and curling along their bottom corners. Some had been spray-painted by the college boys who came from the state's many universities and eyed Enis and his people, in the rare times they saw each other, like common beasts of the field.

So the track, to Enis, brought both good and bad. It brought more of the English world. It brought more of what the English were doing to the world, the same world, after all, of his own people, but a world seen by the English with fallen eyes but by his own people with redeeming ones. *We are the vessel assembled for redemption*, was what Pastor Noblett said of the mission of the Amish. It was no different a covenant than the one God handed to his people in Babylon and Egypt and for which they suffered and were made captive.

For all the money the track brought to his people, Enis never allowed himself to forget their prohibitions; they were guided by the identical sanctions that had ruled their lives since the Days of the Snake. They could not work on the Sabbath. They could not take coffee the English brought in their long containers, nor could they eat the sweet foods that came out of the white bags with paper cups. If a saw or a drill was powered by electricity that came from a cord, they could not use it. If it was powered by a battery, such was permitted, as it was the reaction of Lord-made chemicals, pure things joined by mere proximity to cause a reaction, to make the hand stronger, but with a natural and truthful strength.

Quickness, rapidity, speed. Those things that the English valued so much. It was this that he saw so much of in James, the English that owned the two farms. He talked on a telephone he carried on his belt like a hammer in a joiner's apron. He talked about flights to this and that city, flights that were bringing in shipments of this or that material, none of it—to Enis's mind—seeming to have anything to do with building or repairing things already built.

And James's movements themselves were quick, as though he were the English's very representative, the embodiment of their so-valued velocity. He had come to pay Enis and Noah, which he always did in cash, knowing the boys did not have bank accounts and did not want to take a check to the ledger man at their people's own grange, where it could be changed into money so long as no usury was extracted. James had driven up in the older of his two four-wheel-drive trucks, bounding out like a man about to tell them some welcome news.

But all he was doing was paying them, from the strange wide wallet with a bank's name etched in scarlet letters and with hexlike symbols Enis had seen on Dutch barns in the county north. James shut the truck door and asked them how they were doing in what Enis imagined was a more respectful and measured way than the question would be asked of a fellow English.

This day, James's mottled face was filled with twitches, the slightest of jerks. The long bill of his camouflage cap couldn't hide what seemed to Enis to be these new and possibly anxious, possibly meaningless movements. He usually looked away much of the time that he talked, as if watching the fence line, searching for trespassers. Then, as always, he told the boys to stay out of the whiskey, which made everyone laugh. And then he left.

~

Enis took special care in mounting and climbing the ladders. He remembered what had happened to Toland, a boy who worked in a crew with his brothers and uncles in an area of the country farther south, toward Mount Gilead. Toland was himself far stronger and taller than Enis, who had seen him clamor across roofs and on and off scaffolds with the sureness of a spider. One day, mounting spouting such as this, a rung of Toland's poplar ladder slipped out of its notch and gave way under his boots, pulling him sideways and down, ladder and all, onto the concrete foundation of a well. He'd landed on his head. They said the blood had pooled around his splayed hair in the perfect circle of a halo.

At first, Toland had been unable to move below the shoulders. The English doctors had gotten him exercising in some way, called "therapy," and after a few months, maybe half a year, he'd been taken out of bed and put in a wheelchair. Eventually he got the use of his arms and shoulders back. But Enis saw him at a wedding later in the strange, cold-looking machine, off by himself in a stand of high grass that rose around him like an orange rabbit-trapping basket, his head bent and his eyes closed with regard to the standing world.

Enis thought how much his doubt of sacred things had grown that day. He knew he should have felt pity and charity for Toland, and he could say with clear conscience that he did, some. But some other, uncomfortably bothersome thing crowded into his mind then too. Toland in his chair there on the hilltop was like a hole cut out of the world, the sense of things bulging and wobbling perilously around him for long seconds before tumbling

inside, sweeping away, blowing out through his black silhouette and off into some newly waiting space of absence
and vacancy. Enis felt the sheer, chill draining of it rush
around his heart like loosened ice.

It was then that he had started to slack in the Sunday
meetings. He'd always volunteered to read scripture, for
which his voice was well suited, perfectly suited, like a
blacksmith's watery iron poured into a mold. But now he
held back. Pastor Noblett's eyes waited on him in the call
for volunteers. Enis said nothing, rolling his lips inward,
pressing them with the ridges of his teeth. The blackness of the sight of his friend roiled through his skull
like smoke: the simple, sitting neighbor's revelation of
extinction.

Enis watched Noah out on the barn's high edge,
sweeping away big clumps of hay and brambles from
the old spouting's empty spaces. He remembered the
lace of frozen water hanging from these gutters on a
winter morning catching, as he stood behind it with the
Stanley hammer, the color of the dawn's gray and then
pinkening sky, then the yellow of the sun, then a fire as
whitish as a diamond's luster, and finally the pure blue
of the blazing sky, as blue as he imagined the oceans he
had never seen or even Lake Erie's waters, which may as
well have been as far as an ocean from this place where
he lived.

Such imaginings, he knew, were themselves occasions for sin, or actual commissions of it. The Lord forbade the enjoyment of His beauties independent of their reflection of His Glory, and such was the reason for the studied plainness of Enis's people's dress and speech and all manner of comportment. All of this, this reticence, was a brake on the wheel of the mind, its wildness in the face of beauty, its danger of being drawn in to it like a kind of spell, a drunkenness. But who, since his doubting started, was to say where the love of the thing ended and the love of the Lord in the thing began? He looked at Noah. It was like the borders of the arching rainbow. You saw blue. You saw pink, and you saw orange. But who could point to where the one color met the next, and what two watchers could ever see the same in their seeing?

Enis knew that James was anxious about getting the new spouting up. It was April, the month of rains, and it had to be assembled. It lay along the ground, gunmetal gray, with its stilts and pulleys and ropes wrapped around it like a net. Machines could look as helpless as living creatures. The stilts they now would lift its length with were made of yellow-painted wood with open notches, perfect Y's. Then, once it was hoisted and they got it within a foot or two of the roof edge, it would be jerked to its resting place with pulleys lashed to each of the lightning rods.

Noah motioned Enis down from the ladder, letting

him know it was fine for him to walk a bit or go inside the house to get them water. Enis dismounted the ladder and headed toward the three-sided shed he knew James had put a sink in with his English plumbers.

When he opened the door there was a puzzling busyness to things. There were glass containers with strange-shaped long extensions like bird's beaks and coils that led between containers whose sides were caked with yellow, powdery drippings. Smudged beakers, cracked tubes hung over burners with black, spent matches beside them. And in the corner, oddest of all, were hundreds of squares of green capsules in bubbles that rose off the surface of their silver sheets.

There were piles of powder everywhere, brown orange like the color of ant droppings or termite waste. But they were too neat for the work of animals, threaded the way they were along the table in tiny rows like mold-squared wheat or cones of hand-tamped grain. This was the work of deliberation, he knew, the work of human hands. This was the business, or one of them, that sent the English away and back again, making for the phone chatter, the twitch of worry, the erratic and congested schedules.

Some of the powder must have floated in the air, as there was a metallic taste to it, something that circled his head in a cloudy, acrid mist. Or it could have been the remnants of straw from Noah's pulling. But *something* made him sneeze, and in sneezing, as always, his head shot forward violently. He lost his footing and fell onto the table, stopping himself just in time with the sureness of his builder's hands. But his face ended up right next to a row of piles, face-to-face with them, which caused him to sneeze again. He took in more air, more of the smell, and this time when his head convulsed, his nose and cheeks touched the powder, which he wiped away with great care, especially the bit that was left from what went up his nostrils.

Back on the barn roof, pulling the spouting up on the great ropes, Enis knew that there had been something in the powder he had breathed. At first it was just a tingling in his scalp, the feeling he got after a new hat's fitting, but then a sort of numbness flickered down his neck and traveled along his shoulders with a prickling swiftness. As he turned the pulley's wheel, the sparkle traveled into his elbow, and then his hands, the busiest parts of him, and he felt he could pull his side to the top and into the sheerness of the air itself, and then keep pulling no matter where the pulled thing went, that he could send his left arm over and lift up Noah's side as well. There was a sense of being *ahead* of the cranking, as though the fire in his brain had done it already, was waiting for his flesh to follow through a motion already completed. The lambency was everywhere now, floating out of his bones and muscles and onto the surface of his skin.

After another twenty minutes, the fields of goldenrod began to pulse and undulate, and on the neighbor's lower, brighter properties the light flashed off the windowpanes of chicken houses and tractor mirrors and pools of standing water like torches crackling in a growing darkness. The tops of trees fluttered and sent off tiny waves, soft water ripples into the blue. And looking between his legs and down through the inch-spaced planks, Enis could see strange illuminations in the barn's dank shade: salt blocks that James had stored for deer burned like white clumps of snow; pans left for feeding cats were buffed like coins; and rows of sleeping bats, stretched out like drying shirts, unfolded their tiny pins of eyes, which glittered and then shut again.

Enis clamored over to Noah and grabbed the rope from his hand and pulled. The left side of the hollow metal scoop notched into the eave with a *thock*, and now all they needed to do was screw the rivets in with the battery drills, and they'd be done. Noah was looking at him curiously. Enis scooted down to the roof's edge, pounced out onto the scaffold, and motioned Noah down with the buzzing bit whose trigger he pulled and whose vibration was inside him, or he inside of it. There was no otherness to its happy rattle.

Enis worked so fast now that he was three-quarters of the way through the rivets as he came up to Noah. He went around him and checked his work. Enis was humming a hymn, then singing it almost in a whisper, before he realized his mouth was open. He licked his lips faster, and sweat poured out of his scalp and down the ridges of peach fuzz on his chin. They were done. The spouting was flush against the wide red barn planks now, tight as a fastened harness. They lay on their backs as the scaffold swayed with their weight, and still Enis felt he was moving, felt his heart racing forward and out of his body and into some ambient, shimmering space.

That's when they heard it. The thunder, quite close. Enis thought with satisfaction of their perfect timing, but when he looked at the sky, there were no clouds at all, no darkening masses. It was a wide, still, settled blue.

But out of it the sound still came.

Its bangs poured through the trees at the back of the lot, then another and another. Enis motioned them down the ladders. They shortened the sections and propped them against the barn's foundation. Another boom came through the trees. Two booms cracking, overlapping into a fading echo. Enis ran toward the commotion, ignoring

Noah's calls of caution, motioning him forward through the wrecked arbor and delicate, still rising stands of vines out into the locust grove. Enis got to the fence first and planted his boot on the wire.

The great, brazen cars came over the hill. The first was green—Enis's favorite color—and spotted with letters and signs and the blue silhouette of a flying horse leaping off of the letter *T* and already reaching the *X* at the middle of the word it straddled. The thunder came out of the back of the thing, and there in the turn, just as it slowed itself to a speed that enabled Enis to see it, to truly see it, the sound wound downward like the organ's lowering grumble in church, then sputtered and then wound higher, rising with the clatter of a threshing chain. A great orange car, much flatter and sleeker, was chasing the green one, chomping at its back. Its crouching driver rode through the turn with the same high low revolving growl.

Noah turned away. He lifted his hands as if to push back the great machines, and Enis understood his brother's hesitation, his instinctual revulsion at the devil's larder.

Enis went over and pulled him by the arm. Another car—as blue as a bluebottle fly—tore around the high turn and sent up clouds of dust and smoke as it began its own great calibrations.

Enis patted his brother's broad back. Something was returning to the older brother, not with great weight but a delicate lightness, like a bird settling itself on a branch, on a place that gave promise of peace and of rest. It was all here before him, in this thunder and color: an error-less pattern like falling water. It was a design of man, or of what had made man. The difference didn't seem to matter anymore. It was stopping the hole: the whirling and sucking, the leaking from Toland's chair out into darkness.

Another car came. Its boom filled the grass. Then came another and then another.

THE HOUSE IN BEVERLY HILLS WHERE FAULKNER LIVED

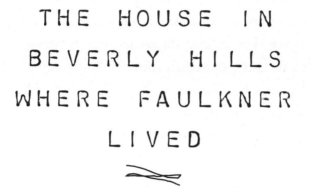

SHIELDS WAS throwing a housewarming party. It was 1988, the year he and all the other young associates in the firm had bought houses. And when you bought a house, this was what you did: You celebrated, you slightly self-congratulated. You let everyone know—with just the right mixture of aloofness and pride—that you were *in*, in without caring that you'd beat the Man at his own game. You kept your deep contempt for property but stepped away from it long enough to create a separate, acquisitive self, nurtured but coldly regarded. A carp in the mammon stream, you fattened but stayed bohemian, flashing your badges of rips and sores.

Shields carried the food out to the long table on his Eel River redwood deck. The sun burned on the bright, trimmed yard; the back house he'd turned into a writing studio; the cyclone fence on the alley bordered with yucca and tiny lime trees. Through the high wall of pines he could see another young striving couple in the adjacent house, oddly or not so oddly unfriendly, preparing for their first baby by building back or up or sideways into whatever space was left in these suddenly valuable war cottage lots. The man was working alone, with a hammer, without contractors. Instead of a nail apron, he kept his tools and water bottle in giant, absurdly pocketed designer shorts that flapped around his knees like a drooping flag.

Seven years before, when the starting gun had ended his ambivalence about law school, Shields literally had to be driven to JFK by his friend and transported on to the plane. Now he had resigned himself to the profession, a scholarly day job, in return for a couple of good hours of writing in the evening. The back house he looked at now was proof of his triumph. It was an island of perfect soundlessness, outfitted with a Selectric and stacks of paper and blue pencils. Its only insulation was a mound of bougainvillea and jacaranda that sparkled on the tarpaper roof like a heap of rubies.

Heather and Xanthippe were the first to arrive. They worked at the branch office of a Boston firm, had attended

Holyoke together, and Shields guessed Xanthippe's father was a classicist. Heather had almond-shaped eyes and black, whiplike hair that fell to the top of her cords. Xanthippe's hair, like her mannerisms, was skittish, jagged, wildly uncontrolled.

"What a *cute* place," she said to him, kissing him on each cheek and maneuvering red wine out of a bag from a high-end Brentwood liquor store. "The deck . . . ," she continued, and behind her Jack could hear Heather gasping at its size, large as the footprint of an additional house.

"This is just what I want," Xanthippe said. "Just exactly."

"Dit-*to*" said Heather, slumping into an Adirondacks chair.

The door banged again while Jack was opening the wine, and in came the Morgan, Lewis crowd: more beauties from the East Coast. Jack knew enough to invite more women than men, that this hallowed party rule applied even more forcefully to the housewarming ritual. It got people out of their partner-pleasing projects, let them know there were good reasons for taking a break from their frantic work pace.

Linda and Diane and Portia put their jackets away in the closet themselves, none of them mentioning that it didn't yet have a door. Linda and Diane were tax mavens, true worker bees who finished off their draftings and closings with cathartic club crawls that took them through half a Sunday night, much like the Japanese with their infamous "water trade." Portia was blond, with hair cut short in a sort of swiveling, floating bowl that static electricity fetched up into imperfect needle clusters. She too was a writer. Her eyes were as blue as lit rock pools. She too had little use for the law outside of it getting her some ocean frontage, a quiet place to get down to the Real Work.

By the time some men arrived, Shields was surrounded by a circle of women. Henschke had come, lumbering and tightly groomed, his arm long enough to wrap itself completely around a case of bottled beer. Tom Patroklas trod in behind him, much easier to take, less serious about himself and the Reagan revolution that was transfiguring so many of them from their liberal pedigrees to a brazen, new, newly selfish unknown. Tom had brought his childhood friend Ben, a neighbor from the Greek section of Queens. His inky Pan curls hooded eyes that were downright reptilian, somehow suited perfectly for the company gobbling that livened his boss's client lists.

The rest were largely unknown to Shields, though some came from his own vast, mirror-lobbied four-floor firm. They came in timidly, blinking, as if just then emerging from their hermit-size offices at the prospect of some social daylight. Again, more women than men. But men there were: young, traditional-looking associates in their button-down flannels; birdly thin, aspiring appellate orators; the weightlifting beach jocks who all lived in the South Bay and who all—with cruel relish— defended personal injury cases, counseling companies whose machines invariably and hideously disfigured people. "Quad crushers," Tom called them.

As was her want, Xanthippe was going off on the pure geographical error of Los Angeles, how she couldn't wait to get back to Northeastern civilization. Shields offered that most people who made that claim ended up staying.

"*Pas moi*," she said. "We're just a box between bridges. I can't wait around for intellectual elevations."

"Yeah, yeah," said Henschke.

"Now that you're in, Jack, hang out a bit, trade up, and cash out," she said.

"I'm with Henschke," said Jack. "Nowhere will be affordable soon. And there's a lot going on here. A lot of stuff moving here. Like Texas in the seventies, but with mountains and rivers."

"Right turn on a red light," said Xanthippe, echoing Woody Allen on Southern California's sole cultural advantage.

"There's more than that," said Jack. "I was just at the house where Faulkner wrote the *To Have and Have Not* screenplay. I mean I drove by it."

"What did *he* say about it?"

"He stayed a long time. A fertile time, I'm told."

"What books?"

"Screenplays."

"Touché."

"He was happy."

"He was *happy*," said Henschke.

Heather leaned forward, sipping a gimlet. "Good place to be starting out," she said. "Practicing. Law."

"It's what we're doin' here, in'it?" said Henschke. Since taking up British football, he had adopted these negative half locutions. All of them fitted his pure, unstudied boorishness.

"What would *you* know about Hellenizing a place, you Reagan robot?"

Xanthippe had smiled when she said it, but Shields saw she was gearing up for him. *Lying in wait* was the phrase they had learned in their homicide classes.

"Sister," Henschke said, "do not engage me." As a wave of groans went across the deck, Shields put his hand in his left pocket, where he'd stuffed the bills the liquor store clerk had given him in change.

"Nobody does pro bono work here either. The firms are worse than the worst New York shops; none of them give a shit about the poor."

"The best thing you can do for *them*," Henschke said, "next to not being one of them, is to make money. Make it and spend it. Spend it on them, hire them for things."

Columns of sun spilled sidelong through the patches of flat pine that formed the wall with the neighbor's deck. From time to time a face came up to one of the holes, and the beam vanished for a second, then came back.

Xanthippe was stacking her olive toothpicks. "Ensure the perpetuation of an underclass," she said. "Keep them cleaning your toilets, your cars."

"Sucking your cocks," said one of the Morgan, Lewis women. She was chain-smoking, stubbing the butts out in a seashell Shields had brought back from a run on the Strand. She wore a dog collar without studs.

Tom's eyebrows shot up. He extended his arms, cracking his fingers. He went inside to make a call.

"The economy is like a bell," Henschke said. "Earnings are pushed or screeded up to a flat point, or a tip, and then the wealth is spread out from there; it ripples out from that space to create new pockets of accumulation, which then flow downward. Quite a lot of wealth, actually."

Quite a lot, really, Shields thought. Something Henschke never would have said before English football.

Portia made a gag-me-with-a-spoon face. Shields admired the long leg she swung over a chair arm. She made the gesture toward Christine, whose eyes half looked at, half rolled at Henschke.

"It happens in every society," he said. "Societies that

succeed, they're driven by it. By self-interest, by . . . individual . . . selfishness."

"To selfishness," said Christine, raising her gin tumbler. "Miss Rand, you are back on the throne."

Len clinked glasses with her. "Selfishness, your hour has come round at last."

Shields could tell there were enough others who agreed with Henschke. Reagan had swept in more than just a conservative revival. All the vitality of youth had been strapped to the engine. The young—whatever else their habits, whatever sex and drugs they did—were throwing aside their New Deal heritage like a collective dirty shirt. Shields saw it as a vast sleepwalking, a hideous, lemminglike somnambulance its practitioners would toss and turn for on their deathbeds.

Tom had come back out with Ben. They resumed their places next to Henschke, as if in solidarity. Henschke sat without expression, smoothing the tops of his pants.

Xanthippe rushed toward Henschke with her empty glass, as if it were a broken-off bottle or a brick. "You fucker. You're just having your day, still riding this anti-Carter tide, and a lot of kids getting outta school and worrying about jobs. But you'll get yours. In the long run, it's guys like you who are in for it."

Inside the French doors, Shields saw people working around a tray. Their movements were surreptitious. The decade before, they would have been chopping cocaine. But as they finished their work, he noticed them dusting off their hands, something unheard of in the days of valuable powders.

Sarah and Bob brought the tray out. Sarah was one of the few married women Shields knew. She was breaking off an affair with the born-again architect redoing her and her husband's house. The architect had installed clear louvers that let in God's goodness, the story went, enlightening her and sending her back to her spouse. (Shields had just bought Mark Strand's new book of poems; in the jacket photo the author sat in his studio under a skylight that let in a single beam, piercing the poet's heart.)

"Something *new*," said Bob, bearing the tray with a limp-wristed flourish. "It's coke that you smoke. Easier on the sinuses."

Three or four long-stemmed pipes lay in a circle on the tray, pastel colored, delicate as dreidls in piles of clay dust. Bob lit the full bowls and passed them out to Claire, Heather, Ben, and the girl Ben was sitting with.

Henschke and Tom shook their heads at an approaching pipe, lifting their bottles.

Shields took a long blast of the one handed to him, and the effect of whatever it was—whatever the brave new, new thing—hit him within seconds, almost before the smoke crossed his tongue and teeth and slid down his throat. The sweet, hot fire of it spilled along the muscles of his neck and shoulders, pulsing, shifting and settling, shifting and settling, like an uncertain, circling creature tamping itself a bed. Compassion, affection—some enormous, convulsive positivity—flowed out of him toward the figures back up on the porch. He felt it, too, toward everything he saw: the mint sprigs and sheep sorrel around the deck's edge, the rotting fronds of the high plantain palm from which his gardener took bananas.

He thought, *like cocaine. A body drug.* But then, it *was* cocaine.

People on the deck stayed in their chairs. No one was going for chips, guacamole, the ancillaries. No one took a second hit from a pipe.

But however still people were, however merged with the furniture, the nonsmokers kept at it. Henschke and Xanthippe stayed at one anothers' throats, Xanthippe gesticulating, throwing up her hands, slicing the air with karate chops.

"How easy it is," she said. "How facile. *The system will take care of itself. The market polices itself.* What a farce."

Henschke sat back on the Adirondacks cushion, hunched up, holding his own.

"There's no 'trickle-down,'" said Xanthippe. Nothing comes down to anybody. It stays with the rich. They sell to *each other*. Each *other*," she said, tottering, leaning. "Are you listening to me? To *one another*."

Henschke lifted his arms in the air again, outlining the bell curve. His pointer fingers traced, the empty bottle dangling from the others.

Shields closed his eyes. He wondered for a second if he'd get the rapid dreams that visit opium users, eaters of yage. But all he saw was a pounding blackness, the heat of the sun sinking into his pores. There were no shapes in the void, no traces, no forms.

He wakened, he thought, within minutes or seconds. But he was new to this stuff, and the time could have been longer.

He had dry mouth, worse than with the worst night of drinking. He took the last sliver of an ice cube out of his bourbon glass. It was beer or soda he needed, one of those flavored ice teas. Portia and Tom came down off the deck and said the same thing. They had cottonmouth. They wanted beer, and the kitchen and ice tubs were empty.

Shields announced a liquor store trip. He wanted to lead it and wanted it to go out the back gate so he could show off the verdancy of the alley, the arresting little starbursts of bougainvillea and jacaranda. He still wanted to exhibit things to visitors. He wanted them to see what Fante had called the Venice alleys, the Alleys of Eden.

People were suddenly gathering around him, everyone wanting to go. He fumbled to find the right key, forcing it into the cyclone fence's ancient rusting padlock. Vines clogged the gate, but the party pushed through with a collective *oomph*, stumbling and settling their feet on the gravel while Shields left the chain's ends dangling and relatched the heavy metal clamp. Shields turned around. He saw how unsteady most of them were and how few of them realized it.

He set out with them across the flattened newspapers and oil-splattered grass toward Lincoln Boulevard. There was a pile of cardboard and rags the crowd of them flowed around, Xanthippe and Heather giving it wide berth and Len stopping for a minute to look down intently at the curled brown corrugated lid flaps and shredded hand towels and milk cartons, a wire cart of some kind giving the feeble mosaic of it all a thrust-up, concave outline it wouldn't otherwise have. Len still held a paper cup of ale, a quarter full, and dropped it in the middle of the pile.

There was a second when the cup's sound, *thock*, slowed everything down, reminding everyone, in every stage of inebriation, just how weirdly balanced their perceptions were. A pool of silence formed around its echo, and slowly, shaking themselves awake, people turned and started walking again.

It was then that the pile started to move.

Something shook inside it. Then it rose upward, whooshing, exploding skyward like a column of water a great stone had been heaved into. Paper and shards of cloth flew off of it, pebbles, strips of foil, sod.

An arm came out. A shirt spread open on the sunburned chest. The chest had boils. The man put his head down and shook it violently, like a dog that had climbed out of a pool. He looked at them, breathing. His face was smeared with wine stains and pitch, and his eyes jerked wildly, watery and white.

The man froze Shields with his stare. Shields had read that most of the homeless were exhausted, famished to the point of psychosis, and that many had gotten to a state where they were too weak to even bend over, to lift things into their mouths.

But the man was looking past Shields, down the length of the alley where the voices were loudest. The entire group of them was running, frantically, their high-held arms waving back and forth. Xanthippe was out ahead of them, curls bouncing, her Mexican peasant blouse flapping on the rear of her jeans. Christine was gaining on her, not looking back. The rest of them scrambled like cats, crisscrossing the alley, racing for the wide, busy safety of the boulevard.

Shields turned back to the man. He thought it was only the two of them there now. But then a foot stepped

out of a bush behind him. It was Henschke, a handker-
chief already in his hand, his other hand reaching in his
jacket pocket for change. Ben was emerging from another
back house's half-open doorway, looking at Henschke and
Shields for an idea of what he should do.

The man sat down on the top of the cart. His breath
was slower now, the panic easing out of his eyes. Shields
stepped toward him, his hand trembling and moistened
with sweat. As if by itself, as if it were somebody else's, it
reached down into his pocket for the bills he hoped were
still there.

SO SLOW IS THE
ROSE TO OPEN

MARGUERITE ENTERED the Martinez Bridge in the brilliant sun that pounded the Bay hills around her, the headlands of Vallejo looming above the rise she was hoping her car would make it over. She sometimes doubted the old Volvo's fitness for this sixty-mile back-and-forth, but now imagined the brightening valley light almost reaching down into the engine to make it surge—a gift of solar voltage given freely by the surrounding mountains. Thinking about it, she realized the car had never really failed her. Hope, surely, had left her at times, but never the workings of this sure machine.

Vinnie was a subject of doubt. Vinnie, light of her life, the grainy speck that fate had blown into her mother's shell and which her grief had rounded like a pearl. The wind buffeted Marguerite up the rising road, and her heart blew open with love. She remembered her daughter's tininess in the crib, the tight, moist grimaces of effort on her pink and yellow face. Some days just laying eyes on her had seemed like an act of faith.

The chug of the methadone buoyed Marguerite now. She saw the silver-black skeleton of the bridge far back below her in the small valley the inlet cut out of the land and remembered she had taken the small pill with a swig of Dr. Pepper just as she drove out from under the bridge's checkered shadow. She clocked the effects of the stuff like that now, in ten-minute, twelve-minute intervals, gauging how much she would feel after only five miles, ten miles of congested freeway driving. Whole patterns and segments of a day could be marked by dropping a scored tablet, washing it down, waiting for the restful, heated wallop of it, like the first minutes of sun on her face when she laid back on a poolside chair. She looked forward to four, which was the earliest she'd ever take a pill. Sometimes it was as early as three, if she had to endure a bottleneck of traffic getting out of the East Bay or needed to steel herself for a particularly mundane test subject interview. She wondered whether her charges even noticed the broad swelling of her pupils, and as she finished the thought, an enormous, blaring truck blew past her, its wake storming in through the passenger window and its driver wincing at her slowness, her smallness in his high, imperious mirror.

When she'd learned of her daughter's autism, and after the first terrors and disbelief had lifted, she started to read. It was her way out of anything, really, her wings out of any labyrinth. And it wasn't just reading, but pouring, devouring—through Brittanicas and journals, the mother's book diaries, through the papers of the specialists she'd started talking to on the vast hillside complex of hospitals they called Parnassus. (Parnassus, that high place, was the Berkeley Hills to her, but it was the San Francisco campus, the med school, that had taken that name.)

It turned out to be easier when her husband left, as she had heard it would be from others in her support group. She no longer had to tolerate his mindless optimism, his generalized nonsense about Vinnie's probable interior bliss, her consciousless states and planes of happiness. Marguerite had to work harder with him gone, but gladly took the trade-off of real, measurable progress with Vinnie—a sense of what could be learned and what could be counted as true improvement.

She would wake in the night now to hear Vinnie cry, and in those moments could not remember her husband's name. Marguerite had wondered—but not too much—whether his methadone treatments were what had given him his newfound, chatty obliviousness. This question, plus the desire for relief from fights with him, started her pilfering the small, white ovals by twos and threes as the skirmishes got worse. She conserved them, scoring and slicing them with Stanley knives and, if necessary, breaking off fragments, watching the plumes of their powder settle into the wetness of her palm and dissolve in satiny lines.

The late-afternoon sun had tipped the wheat fields orange. The land was flattening out, and soon the Tinkertoy houses of the bus stop and diner towns would appear in the brown: Vacaville, Dixon, Winters, Yolo. On both sides of the freeway, long ribbons of road ran even with the four-land blacktop. Produce trucks and farm equipment ran along them in all directions through the sea of grass.

The house in Davis had been refitted with a settlement Marguerite had gotten from one of Vinnie's early treating doctors. It had ramps for the wheelchair when Vinnie needed it, fortified windows, a fence to keep her back from the menacing roads her mother looked out on now.

There were bicameral and unicameral autisms, she'd learned from the Parnassus doctors. Unicamerals were most common—a child's whole world blurred and confused but for one clear tunnel into brilliance, one arcane talent like mathematics or baroque music. The bicamerals like Vinnie were rarer. *Two* things were what they entered and bridged together to make their world cohere.

But they found their tunnels slowly, a mistake at a time, unlike the unicamerals who came developed and perfect and full.

Marguerite was still dumfounded by the early midcentury view of autism as a failure of affectionate mothering. Though the doctors had ridiculed the school, from Bettelheim to Kety to Tinbergen and his gulls and laboratory monkeys, Marguerite was haunted by its long, compelling grip on the parade of giant minds. What if there was something to the notion of the bad mother cause, and the view that "super mothering," like intensive hugging, formed the ostensive cure? Hadn't she done all that she could? Tinbergen had said in his Nobel speech that, "In saying this, we are not blaming these unfortunate parents." The current trend was to burn this tradition out of the history of psychiatry, but panic flooded through her in moments like these, icy water, rippling and searing her lungs.

Two camerals. Two avenues. What Kanner, in his breakthrough paper, "Autism,"—*autistic, autism* from the Greek for *self*—had written of seeing in the children he studied, music lovers first but at the same time players with worms and frogs and salamanders, which they picked up with bright toy pails and threw on things in no particular order. Vinnie certainly loved music: Satie and show tunes and the AM radio Aerosmith that Marguerite had gratefully missed in the seventies. And for Vinnie, the fauna

of choice were snails: the reliable, dew-covered, monotonous garden snails of the Sacramento Valley. Marguerite
had seen her hundreds of times watching the creatures'
heads craning and twisting in and out of their shells. Vinnie picked them up and peered at them, turning them in
her hand like patterned leaves before resting them gently
in the bottom of her bucket.

Somehow the thought of them now, on the spades and
on the handles of hoes, on the shed's foundations, brought
the air's white chill back into Marguerite's heart. It was
dread that she felt, pure and simple dread. Vinnie's fasci-
nation for the dank things did not jive with her coy love
of melody, though her mother knew the starkness of the
opposing interests was what made for the subject's psychic
balance, "equilibrium" the paper had stated, "through the
fusing of contraries." But now the snail chasing seemed
only an aberration of her daughter's thought: a magnet
for the soiled and vile, drawing the little girl's lightness
down, in Marguerite's mind, to something underground.

And Vinnie's outbursts had gotten worse; she was
more volatile now, especially in her evening greetings of
her mother. She would beat on the bucket bottoms and
shake dog chains when Marguerite first got out of the
car, circling, hedging around her mother before walking
over warily to greet her. One day, just before Marguerite
pulled up, Vinnie had thrown dog shit over the fence at

a neighbor's house. Marguerite rolled her window down to see Vinnie leaning against a plank with her face buried in her hands, the babysitter Lupe standing in silhouette before the affronted party, her head bowed in exaggerated contrition.

Marguerite had upped her methadone doses then, to what she had taken today: an entire pill, unbroken, unabridged. She didn't feel terrible about taking this much, and in fact the thrust, the push, the *roll* of it arrived much more forcefully when she "wholed," her blood feeling crowned and brimming as its warmth washed outward, racing through her limbs like electric light along its skin of tungsten. But driving on it was making her more and more anxious now. Once, with Vinnie in the car, she had backed into her parking space and clipped a pole with the driver's side mirror. It shattered with a soft, explosive sparkle, a shard or two slipping out of the casing to tinkle on the echoing cement. Vinnie frowned as though she would start to cry but only gazed at the mirror and now always came back to it, reaching up toward the web of fractures until her hand could be stopped.

The Davis exit was banked immensely with white violets and peonies, usually a glad flag of homecoming on these long afternoons of driving. But when Marguerite came off on to the frontage road by the veterinary barns her heart sank again. She had the sense of another disaster waiting for her at the rented house she'd never salvaged from the mess in which she'd taken it over from a colleague. These slab houses, all pastel stucco and crumbling second roof, had a way of sinking into the blacktopped streets and coral trees and mud-colored grass they sat in. You could do nothing but bide your time in them until tenure. You were *young* faculty. These were your houses. Their ticky-tacky was part of the dues you paid.

She knew Lupe would be irritated at her lateness. She couldn't kid herself. All day cooped up with Vinnie had maddened her many times. The endless circling of rooms, the humming of bars of songs from *Annie*, the gathering up of sticky things from the ground. It would tax you and drag you out and then tear you up or melt you down.

When she turned onto her street, the slant of the light was high and clear, but nothing could lift the despair of waiting for her own house. She counted off the colored doors and chipped siding, the sandy, treeless yards full of toys. Fear flashed up her back again as the front of her house came into view.

Something was on it. Huge clusters of specks. It looked like hundreds, packed closely in what had originally been columns. How had whoever put them there done it? Where had they found the patience and time?

But there was something different about this group— their closeness, a pattern, a graceful molding of shape.

They had moved, somehow, in the same direction, and the waning light caught the glint of their slime. The top group had left behind a giant, right-leaning *I*, and below it were letters she squinted to see.

Love, said their traces, flickering pale pink. They were moving down toward the more recently made group, which was dark, still intact, too new to have roamed. The right top of the *U* was unfinished, abandoned. Vin must have heard the car when she was finishing the letter and run inside.

Marguerite wheeled the car into the drive and stopped. She leaned back and looked at the wall through her tears, touching her cheeks and the drops on her blouse. Through the blur her calmed eyes simply followed the shells, the antennae still wiggling and pulling them on. They moved slow as a clock hand, invisibly moving, the great letters blazing in the afternoon sun.

ACKNOWLEDGMENTS

Early readers of these stories were abundant, generous, and insightful. Thanks to Anthony Robinson, Ken Dekleva, Dean Ferguson, Lani Perlman and other fellow staffers at *Transformation*; the astonishing Laura Mazer; Deborah Bauman; Mitchell Albert; Laura Frankena; Stephen Andrew; Eric Berkowitz; Jennifer Gray; Jennifer Breitinger, Jane Drake and Janet Herman; Atom Egoyan; James Elkins; Michael Cunningham; Nick Flynn; Erin Hosier and Henry Dunow at Dunow, Carlson; George Soneff and Ann Kelly; Victoria Pynchon; John Witte; Daniel Bourne; Billy Fontenot; Carolyn Rossip Malcolm; Speer Morgan; Tom Shields; Ralph Savarese; Carolyn Issa and Masoud Golsorki; Samantha Gillison; Emily Moore; David Katz; Paul Sandburg;

Robert W. Lewis; William Giraldi, Stuart Dybek; Lisa Skaist; Abdel Shakur; Matt Weiland at *The Paris Review*; Michael Signorelli; Anna Wilson; Antoine Wilson; Maya Wirick; Karen Gottesman and Nancy Gottesman.

As always, immense gratitude to Malu Halasa, friend, advisor and U.K. agent.

To everyone at Counterpoint and Soft Skull, profuse thanks, especially (again) Laura Mazer, Denise Oswald, Jack Shoemaker, Charlie Winton, Mikayla Butchart, Carrie Dieringer, and Tiffany Lee. To Domini Dragoone, painter of the poppy blossom.

Some facts about crime/suicide scene clean-ups were taken from the book *Gig* by John and Marisa Bowe and Sabin Streeter (Three Rivers 2001). Events forming a basis for "The Way It Came" were taken from a California Highway Patrol emergency tape recording in 1996. Some of the research used for "Angel of Sleep" came from Ralph Quinones and other drug beat reporters of *The Los Angeles Times* and *The New York Times*, too numerous to mention, and from Nick Reding's *Methland* (Bloomsbury 2009) as well as Josh Lyon's *Pill Head* (Hyperion 2009). Martin Booth's *Opium* (St. Martins 1996) was also a vital historical source.

"Hardin Street," first picked from the slush pile at *Kiosk* by his editors, is for the late Leslie Fiedler. "Getting Hector," written as it was in the Luxor Hotel's pyramid with him in reluctant attendance, is dedicated to my son, Evan. "Scorpion Days" is for Anthony Robinson, with whom it would have been a pleasure to share a life sentence in a Moroccan prison, though we did not need to. "Self-Portrait With Wounded Eye" takes its title from a triptych by Francis Bacon. "Undertow" is derived from and contains quotations, or near-quotations, from "Skunk," a story in Geoff Dyer's *Yoga for People Who Can't Be Bothered to Do It*, published by Pantheon and Vintage (special thanks to Eric Simenoff at William Morris/Endeavor). "So Slow Is The Rose to Open" is a line from Pound's *Cantos*, and the conceit of the story was suggested to me by the poet Sandra McPherson shortly after the birth of my twins.

These stories, sometimes in somewhat different form, appeared in the following periodicals, and grateful acknowledgment is given to their editors: *Kiosk:* "Hardin Street"; *Transformation:* "Getting Hector"; *Folio, The Baltimore Review:* "The Way It Came"; *Northwest Review:* "Scorpion Days" and "Road Out Of Babylon"; *Santa Monica Review:* "Angel of Sleep"; *Fiction:* "Undertow"; *Quarterly West, Cimarron Review:* "Peaceable Kingdom"; *Florida Review:* "Self-Portrait With Wounded Eye"; *Louisiana Review:* "Toland's Chair" and "The House In Beverly Hills Where Faulkner Lived." "Road Out Of Babylon" was made into a radio play on the BBC Program Four, retitled "Blood and Guts."

Photo: Ken Weingart

Richard Wirick's first book of linked stories, *One Hundred Siberian Postcards,* was released to wide acclaim in 2007. His other stories and articles have appeared in a number of publications, including *The Los Angeles Times, Playboy, Fiction, Chicago Review, L.A. Weekly, Northwest Review,* and *PEN Quarterly.* He lives in Southern California.